Herby's SECRET FORMULA

Written & Illustrated by **Sue C. Hughey**

Sue C. Hughey

Associated Arts Publisher
Grand Junction, CO

First edition
Printed in the United States of America

Library of Congress Control Number: 2008941351

ISBN: 978-0-9814539-5-8

Cover art by Sue Hughey
All illustrations by Sue Hughey

Published by:
Associated Arts
536 Tiara Dr.
Grand Junction, CO 81507
970-241-8024
suehughey@earthlink.net

In association with:
Lifetime Chronicle Press
121 N. Park Ave.
Montrose, CO 81401
970-240-1345
chronicle@montrose.net

Dedicated to my dear sons,
Jeff and Greg Hughey

Table of Contents

Chapter 1

Herby's Experiment

Whoopeee!!! yelled Herby. It's happening!

Bozo, Herby's dog, looked up at his master and quizzically cocked his head.

"Look here, Bozo, the fish are getting smaller. That chemical I just tried made them shrink even more."

"Herby!" came a yell from downstairs, "Get down here right now!"

Bozo whined.

"You're right, Bozo. He sounds angry."

"Be right there, Dad!"

Herby threw a dust cover over the vials and beakers on his lab table.

He ran down the hallway and down the stairs, with Bozo bounding after him.

As he hurried across the dining room to take his place at the table, Herby was surprised to see his favorite aunt there. "Hi, Aunt Bert! I didn't know you were coming to dinner."

"Be right there, Dad!"

Before she could respond, Herby's dad sternly said, "Young man, you know not to be late for dinner."

"Sorry. I was busy with an experiment."

"I do wish you'd pay more attention to the time, Herby," said Mom. I think if it weren't for school and your Boy Scout activities, you'd never leave your room."

Herby ducked his head and looked at his reflection in his plate.

Dad picked up a plate of pot roast and handed it to Aunt Bert. "Help yourself, Roberta, and pass it on."

"So what has you so busy up there in that spooky room of yours, Herby?" asked Aunt Bert.

"He's trying to shrink stuff," Herby's little sister, Suzanne, giggled.

"Shrink stuff?" asked Aunt Bert, "Like what?"

Herby glared at his sister. "You little snoop! I told you to stay out of my room! You've been messing with my tape recorder again, haven't you?"

"That's enough, you two!" snapped Dad.

"But, Dad! She could ruin my whole experiment!"

"I'll deal with your sister. Right now, I want you to both shut your mouths and eat."

"Dad," said Herby, "Do you realize that's a physical impossibility?"

"Hi, Aunt Bert! I didn't know you were coming to dinner."

Everyone laughed.

After dessert, Suzanne asked to be excused from the table. "Yes, you may," answered Dad. "Go straight to your room and go to bed."

"Go to bed?" she wailed. "It's too early."

"Not for little girls who don't do as they're told. You were told to stay out of Herby's room. Now go to bed."

With her little face screwed into a frown, Suzanne left the table. Herby watched her slowly climb the stairs, dramatically clinging to the banister and whimpering as she went.

"Dad," Herby asked, "Can I get a lock on my door? She's going to do it again. I just know she will. If I can win the county science fair, I'll have a chance at the state science fair. All that is just too important to get messed up by some little busybody snoop."

"We'll see about a lock when your mother and I get back from our trip."

"Trip?" Herby asked. "What trip?"

"I have business in Orlando, Florida, in a few days. We've decided to extend the trip and take a short vacation."

"Aunt Bert is going to stay with you and Suzanne while we're gone," Mom added. "She came over tonight so we could show her a few things around the house."

I hope they don't show her how to use the stove, thought Herby. *She's really cool for an aunt, but not so hot as a cook.*

"Won't we have fun, Herby?" Aunt Bert asked. "Is

there anything special you'd like to do?"

"We could go out to eat," Herby quickly answered.

Mom got up from the table. "Excuse me while I go upstairs to check on Suzanne."

"Go right ahead," said Aunt Bert. Herby and I will clear the table and take care of the dishes. Thanks for another wonderful meal. I wish I were as good a cook as you."

So do I, thought Herby.

Dad picked up some dishes and headed for the kitchen. "I volunteer to scrub that heavy roasting pan."

As they worked, Aunt Bert said to Herby, "You never did tell me what your science project is. What is it you're trying to shrink?"

"Ummm—I have a lot more work to do and tests to run," he answered.

"I understand, but can't you give me a little hint?"

"Well—it's got to do with saving the world."

"Saving the world? From what?"

"From one of this planet's greatest threats, Aunt Bert, overpopulation."

"Overpopulation? I know it's a big problem, but how is your experiment going to affect that?"

Aunt Bert set the dishes on the counter. Dad stopped scrubbing the roasting pan and turned to hear Herby's answer.

"There are just way too many people for the earth to support. And millions more are born every year. There's not enough land, food, or water for them all. We learned about all that in Social Studies class. And

5

look at all the animals that are going to be extinct, and some that already are, just because people have taken over their habitats. So I figure that if all the people and all the animals were a whole lot smaller, they would need less food, and there would be plenty of room for all of them."

Herby hadn't meant to go into such detail about his plan, especially at such an early stage in his experiments. He looked at his aunt and then at his father. He could tell by the look on their faces that he had said too much.

"And you think it's possible to make them all smaller?" Dad asked. "To SHRINK them?"

"Well—it's got to do with saving the world."

6

"Yes, Sir."

"Is that what you've been wasting your time on up there day after day?"

"Yeah, Dad, but it's not a waste of—"

Dad interrupted. "I assumed you were working on something worthwhile. I appreciate your concern for the whole world, Herby, but if you plan to win any science fairs, you have got to get serious."

Herby's mom entered the kitchen. "Looks like most of the work is done in here. Why don't we all go to the living room now and relax?"

"You three go on," said Herby. "I'll finish loading the dishwasher."

"Why, thank you," said Mom, somewhat surprised.

"Fine," Dad said, "but we'll finish this conversation later, Herby."

Herby didn't like doing dishes, but it was better than arguing with his dad about his experiment. His parents had thought it was great that he wanted to enter the science fair. They had even bought him the expensive laboratory equipment he'd asked for. He felt that he just couldn't let them down. But he also felt that his current project was even more important than winning a science fair. He knew his plan for saving the world sounded hard to believe. That's why, until now, he'd been so secretive.

Me and my big mouth, thought Herby. *I'm SO CLOSE to the answer. I'm positive the goldfish are smaller. I measured them carefully and made careful*

7

notes. They are definitely smaller, but not enough.

After turning on the dishwasher, Herby went into the living room and announced, "I have a lot of homework to do, so I'd better get to it."

"Do you have so much homework that you can't spend a little time in here with us?" Aunt Bert asked.

Herby's mother answered for him. "Children have a lot more to learn than when we were in school, Bert. You and Herby will have plenty of time to spend together in a few days."

"I'll see you Friday, Aunt Bert," Herby said.

"Just don't be up there piddling with that so-called science project of yours instead of doing your homework," Dad said.

"Goodnight, everyone," said Herby.

"Goodnight," they all answered at once.

Feeling dejected, Herby climbed the stairs with Bozo close behind. His dad's words echoed in his mind, "A piddling, so-called science project." *I'll show them,* thought Herby. *After I win the Nobel Peace Prize, Dad will be eating those words!*

When he walked past Suzanne's door, he heard her jumping on the bed. He banged on her door and yelled, "You're supposed to be in bed, you little snoop!"

Suzanne kept bouncing as she called out, "I AM in bed, you silly scientist." She kept up a chant as Herby walked down the hallway to his room, "Sil-ly, sil-ly, sci-en-tist. Sil-ly, sil-ly, scientist."

Chapter 2

The Formula

Although it was still August, Herby had looked forward to the start of school. But for the next two days, he had trouble paying attention in his classes. The only thing he could think about was his experiment. He went over and over it in his mind, trying to think of what ingredients were needed to perfect his formula. He even considered going to Mr. Devers, the science teacher, to see if he had any ideas. But after the reaction his dad had to his experiment, he decided against it. Mr. Devers might also think his idea was unrealistic.

He was still deep in thought when his friend, J.C., waved his hand in front of Herby's face. "Hey! Wake up. It's three o'clock. The bell rang. It's Friday, and school's out."

"Oh." Herby came out of his trance.

As they walked to the bicycle racks, J.C. said, "Herby, your mind seems to be in outer space. Do you remember the picnic on Sunday?"

The picnic! thought Herby. *I forgot all about it. I even forgot to tell Mom and Dad.*

His scout troop was holding a picnic for all the new scouts and their families. Herby decided not to mention it to his parents. He was afraid they might cancel their short vacation to attend.

They don't get to take a vacation by themselves very often, he thought. And I'd better not mention it to Aunt Bert until Sunday. She might want to fix potato salad or something. I'll leave just enough time for us to pick up hot dogs and stuff at the store.

Herby's dad was loading a suitcase into the car as Herby peddled into the driveway.

"Hi, Dad."

"Hi, sport! I'm glad you're home. Your mother and I will be leaving in just a few minutes."

Mom shut the door and hurried down the porch steps. As she leaned over to hug Herby, he kissed her on the cheek. She was wearing perfume. "You smell really good, Mom."

"Thanks, sweetie. Now remember—"

Herby listened politely, but didn't pay much attention as his mother repeated the same instructions she had given him before.

"Agnes will be here about four o'clock. She's the best cleaning lady we've ever had, and I don't want to lose her. Make sure every creepy crawly thing in your room is put away and covered up before she gets here."

"I will, Mom. You'd better hurry so you won't miss your plane."

Dad hugged him around the shoulders. "We know you'll take good care of things. I realize Suzanne can be a pest, but please try to be patient with your little sister."

"Aunt Bert will be here as soon as she picks Suzanne up from her dance lesson," added Mom. "Be ready, and wear something nice. She wants to take you out instead of cooking."

"That's a relief," said Herby.

"We'll be back on Thursday evening," Mom continued. "Please be polite and eat whatever Bert cooks for you."

"Don't worry. I'll feed some to Bozo first. If he thinks it's okay, I'll eat it."

Mom grinned at his little joke.

Herby waved as his parents' car backed down the driveway. "Have a good time," he called.

As he let himself in the front door, Herby could hear Bozo whining and barking at the back door. Herby joined him in the backyard to play fetch for a while. Finally, Herby said, "Come on, Boy, we've got work to do."

The two of them climbed the outside stairs that led from the backyard patio to Herby's room. Herby loved the roomy old house. It had been in his family for several generations. His grandparents, who had moved to Arizona, had previously owned the house. He especially loved his big room, which had once been his grandmother's studio. She used to give art lessons there, and the outside entrance and stairs were built for her students' use. Besides having many windows that let in lots of light, the room contained a sink. That made it a perfect science laboratory.

Herby entered his room and glanced at the clock on the wall. Agnes would be here any minute to clean the house. He looked around to see what needed to be done to get ready for her. He put all the jars that were filled with dissected specimens on one shelf. On the cloth that he covered them with, he pinned a note that read "Do not remove or you will throw up." He then began covering the small-animal cages on the other shelves. The white mice were all piled on top of one another, sleeping soundly. Mrs. Gerbil was feeding her most recent brood. In the adjacent cage, Mr. Gerbil raced furiously on his exercise wheel. The next cage was empty and the door open.

Herby got down on his knees to look under the furniture. "Come on, Hairy, where did you go this time?"

"Wake up, Bozo. Find Hairy."

The old dog got up slowly, stretched, sniffed, and then walked stiffly to the bed. With his nose, he raised the bottom of the bedspread. The fat little hamster was hiding in one of Herby's slippers.

"Thanks Boy." Herby grabbed the small furry creature and then got to his feet.

He noticed that his pet bull snake, Wilma, was stretched out on the floor against one wall, sunning herself. He had rescued Wilma from some boys who were trying to kill her with a hoe. They thought she was a rattlesnake. Herby had been working on his

Reptile and Amphibian Merit Badge in scouts at the time and knew she was a harmless bull snake. The hoe had chopped up Wilma pretty badly, but Herby was able to nurse her back to health. She was a little crooked here and there and always would be.

Herby picked up the snake with his free hand and then said to the hamster, "Hairy, it's a good thing for you that I fed Wilma this morning, or she might have had you for lunch."

After putting the animals away, he stopped to study the bowl of goldfish. *They appear to have shrunk even more,* he thought. *I'll measure them again later.* He was happy to see that their shrinking didn't seem to affect their good health.

Herby carefully picked up the glass chemistry flask that held his precious formula. *Where can I put this so it won't get knocked over?* He thought of several places, but each time he set it down, Herby pictured Agnes knocking it over with her duster. Looking at his small refrigerator, he thought, *I don't think she'd dust in there, but the cold might adversely affect the formula.*

There seemed to be only one thing to do. He would keep the formula with him until Agnes had finished cleaning his room. With his flask in one hand and his clean clothes under his arm, he started down the hallway to the bathroom. He heard Agnes let herself in the front door and call, "I'm here."

Herby peered over the banister. "Hi, Agnes. I'm going to take a bath. I'll be out of your way if you want to start in my room. Everything's ready for you in there."

"Everything?"

"Yes, Ma'am. All the critters are locked securely in their cages and covered up. You won't even know they're there."

"I certainly hope not," answered Agnes as she headed up the stairs with the vacuum cleaner.

At the sight of the vacuum cleaner, Bozo hunkered down and followed Herby into the bathroom. Herby set the flask on the edge of the bathtub in the corner. He turned on the water and poured a generous amount of bubble bath into the tub. It was a family rule that, after bathing, each person must leave the tub clean. He didn't particularly like the bubble bath's overly sweet smell, but his scientific mind had noticed that it helped prevent the formation of a bathtub ring. Usually, the dirt could just be rinsed down the drain with the bubbles, and the tub needed very little scrubbing.

Herby settled down into the white foamy mass and rested his head on the back of the tub. He studied the flask at the foot of the tub and began thinking about its contents. *Spilling those particular chemicals into the goldfish bowl was pure luck. That accidental discovery could save the world. But I need to keep experimenting to make the fish much smaller.*

While lost in thought, Herby also lost track of time. His pondering was interrupted by the sound of his aunt's voice coming from downstairs. "Hi, Agnes. Is Herby ready to go?"

Aunt Bert! She couldn't be here already! thought
Herby as he struggled to sit up in the slippery tub.
"OH, NO!" Slipping, he felt his heel hit the flask
containing his formula and saw it tumble into the mass
of bubbles.

Herby grabbed under the water for the flask
and accidentally knocked the plug out of the drain.
He frantically felt around until he found the flask
but couldn't seem to get his hands around it. The
washcloth that had been draped over his knee was now
huge and weighing him down. As he struggled to get
free from it, he felt himself sucked into a whirlpool.
Swirling around and around over the drain, he yelled

"OH, NO!"

with delight, "I'm shrinking! The missing ingredient to my formula is in the bubble bath! Oh, my gosh! I'm SHRINKING! HELLLLP!"

"I'm SHRINKING! HELLLLP!"

Chapter 3

A Long Way Down

Herby struggled furiously to pull himself free of the whirlpool, but the force of the swirling water was too much for him. As he slipped into the drain, he looked up to see a puzzled Bozo peering down at him. The sound of the dog's frantic barking faded away as Herby was swept deep into the pipe. He was carried swiftly along but gradually felt less and less water around him. He coughed out some bubbles and gasped for breath. But there was very little air to breathe. He pushed against the stinking, slimy pipe, trying to slow himself down. *If I get into the main sewer, I'll be a goner for sure,* thought Herby.

He was on his back, pushing hard against the pipe, when his arms suddenly shot up into an opening. It was another pipe vertical to the one he was in. He held on tightly and slowly worked the rest of his body into it until he could stand up.

It was another pipe vertical to the one he was in.

At least there's more air. I can breathe again! he thought. *And this pipe isn't slimy.* He rested while mulling over his predicament.

Suddenly he remembered a movie he had watched when he was working toward his Climbing Merit

Badge. In the film, members of a mountain climbing expedition had worked their way up an ice crevasse by pressing against its sides. Herby backed against the pipe and lifted his feet to press against the other side. *Well, here goes. It's do or die*, he thought as he began working his way up.

As he slowly ascended, the darkness gradually gave way to light, and he could see blue sky

It's do or die he thought as he began working his way up.

above. He was in one of the vent pipes protruding from the roof of the house. He was afraid to look down. He didn't want to think about how far he would fall if he slipped.

Herby occasionally stopped to rest his trembling muscles and to catch his breath. He rested one leg at a time, dangling it while the other leg held him fast against the pipe. He guessed that the climb to the top was probably only fifteen or twenty feet. But in his small condition, it was like climbing a hundred feet.

After what seemed like hours, Herby reached the top, exhausted. Breathing hard, he hung over the edge of the vent pipe by his armpits and looked down to the roof. *That's a long way down*, he thought. The metal gutter that ran along the edge of the roof was nearby. It was filled with leaves, and some had backed up around the vent. *I'd better not miss*, he thought. *Those rough, asphalt shingles could skin me alive.*

He pulled himself out of the pipe and, hanging onto its top, walked himself down the outside as far as he could. Looking down, he took a deep breath and let go. When he felt his feet touch, Herby relaxed his body, rolling through the leaves and into the gutter. His knees and elbows were skinned a little, but the leaves had softened the fall.

Sitting among the leaves, he tried to collect his thoughts. His mind seemed to be in a fog. *I hope my brain didn't shrink more than the rest of me.*

After a while, his head began to clear, and his stomach growled. He looked over the edge of the gutter at the lawn far below. Herby noticed a vine that had grown over the gutter and attached itself to the roof shingles. Plowing through the leaves, he made his way over to the vine and got a good grip on it. He climbed out of the gutter and began the long descent. The branching leaves and flowers, and the trellis itself, made a good ladder.

He was making good progress when there was a sudden ear-splitting humming behind him. Turning around, he found himself staring into the eyes of an angry-looking hummingbird. The bird's long slender bill looked like a sword to Herby, and he quickly slipped behind a slat of the trellis. *I hope it's just curious and not trying to protect a nearby nest. It could run me clean through with that bill.* After darting back and forth a few times to look him over, the bird zoomed away much to Herby's relief.

He started down again, and then stopped to listen. This time he heard a deafening buzzing! It sounded like several chain saws all going at once.

Bees! The trumpet vine is full of them! The poison from just one sting could kill me.

Herby tried to stay calm. His progress now became quite slow. Whenever he came near a cluster of flowers where bees were working, he stood still and waited until each bee had its fill and buzzed away.

This is taking so long, he thought. *I hope I can get down before dark!*

When he finally reached the ground, Herby could hear the sobbing voice of his aunt coming from around

*...he found himself staring into the eyes of an
angry-looking hummingbird*

the corner of the house. Making his way toward her
voice, he avoided the deep grass by taking a short
cut through the flower bed. Walking over the dirt
barefooted was like walking over a field of boulders.
The leaves of the flowers, as he brushed past them, felt
like sandpaper against his bare skin.

While looking at a Mountainview Police car
parked in front of the house, he stumbled over
something. It was an old garden glove. Herby picked it
up and shook the dirt out of it. Most of the fingertips
were worn through. Concerned about his nakedness,
he stepped into the glove.

He slipped his feet into two of the fingers, and
one arm into the thumb. The glove made walking slow
and awkward, but he didn't want to make a spectacle
of himself. The situation was already embarrassing
enough.

Herby rounded the corner of the house. He was
still some distance away, but could see a group of
people on the front porch. There was his Aunt Bert
and Suzanne, the elderly couple from next door, two
policemen, and Agnes, the cleaning lady.

One of the policemen was writing something in
a little notebook. "What makes you so sure he's been
kidnapped?" he asked. "He may have just gone to visit a
friend."

Aunt Bert sobbed. "His glasses were left beside
the bathtub. He needs them to read. He never goes
anywhere without them."

"Can you tell me what he was wearing?"

"He's been kidnapped . . ."

"NOTHING," cried Bert. "The clothes you saw on the stool beside the bathtub were the ones he was planning to put on after his bath. The ones he took off were still lying on the floor." She then broke into sobs and began wailing loudly.

Poor Aunt Bert. I've never seen her so worked up! Herby continued toward the porch, but was slowed down by having to make his way through several large clumps of flowers.

He heard the policeman say to Agnes, "I understand you were the last person to see the boy. Did you see anyone else in the house?"

"No, sir. I had just gone to the front door to greet his aunt here, when we both heard the dog barking upstairs. We thought maybe the dog had gone into

Herby's room and was barking at one of Herby's little animals. So we just kept talking for a while and didn't pay much attention. When I went back upstairs to finish cleaning, I could tell the barking was coming from inside the bathroom. I knocked on the door. When Herby didn't answer, I peeked in and he was gone. Just VANISHED!"

"He's been kidnapped," wailed Aunt Bert, "right out of the bathtub in his own home!"

Thrashing through the flowers, Herby called out, "I'm not kidnapped, Aunt Bert! Look down here! Can't you see I'm here?" But no one heard his cries.

"Stay calm, ma'am," said one of the policemen. "Where are his parents? Have they been notified?"

"They're on their way to Florida," answered Bert. "I left word with the airline to have them return immediately."

"Good. Stay by the phone, and don't let anyone go upstairs. It's off limits until the crime lab can get here in the morning."

"It's a good thing you hadn't cleaned much of the house yet," he said to Agnes. "The crime lab needs to have everything left exactly as it was."

As the policemen were leaving, one turned back to Bert. "This photograph of him should help a lot," he said. "How old did you say he is?"

"He's nearly twelve," answered Bert. "But he's small for his age."

She's got that right, thought Herby, as he thrashed through another clump of flowers.

"Look down here! Can't you see I'm here?"

Still struggling to reach the front porch, Herby thought, *Now, I've done it. Mom and Dad were looking forward to this trip, and now I've spoiled it for them.*

The elderly neighbors, Mr. and Mrs. Duffy, were still standing on the front porch. "Would you like to come in?" Aunt Bert asked.

"Thank you dear," Mrs. Duffy answered, "but it's getting dark, and we'd best get home. Let us know if we can do anything, Roberta—anything at all."

"I will," answered Bert through her tears. "I'll turn on the porch light so you can see to get home."

Exhausted, Herby finally made it to the front walk. He looked up just in time to see his aunt closing the front door. He cried, "Wait, Aunt Bert! Here I am! Please, don't close the door! Aunt Bert!"

When the porch light came on, Herby knew his cries would not be heard. He then turned toward the Duffy's, who were crossing the lawn to their home. "Mr. Duffy! Mrs. Duffy! Please come back!"

He heard Mrs. Duffy say, "It's so strange, dear, I can almost hear the little angel's voice."

"Little angel? That's not what you called him when you found him with his pet snake in your vegetable garden."

Herby yelled after them at the top of his tiny lungs. "I was doing you a favor! Wilma was eating up all those beetles you'd been complaining about."

Mrs. Duffy stopped and turned around. Herby jumped up and down, waving his arms and calling to her. She turned back and said to Mr. Duffy as they continued home, "Yes, I can almost hear his voice."

It was completely dark by the time Herby had climbed the porch steps, using the bricks alongside as hand and footholds. He lay exhausted at the top of the steps, hoping with all his might that Aunt Bert would open the door. He felt weak from hunger and from the rigors of the day.

Just as he was about to doze off, a huge mosquito landed on him. He jumped to his feet and waved his arms to ward it off. He looked up and saw dozens of mosquitoes and other insects buzzing about. *They're attracted by the porch light. I've got to find cover!* He spotted the recycling bins beside the front door. *I was supposed to take those out to the curb for pickup in the morning.* Herby ran to the bins.

Knowing he couldn't climb the bin's plastic-mesh side while wearing the stiff glove, he stepped out of it. After reaching the top of the bin, he looked over the various bottles and jars inside. *There's one that should provide some protection, but it's sure going to be cold and uncomfortable in there.* He looked over at the adjacent bin that held discarded newspapers and had an idea. Slipping and sliding, he made his way across the glass containers to the newspapers. He tore off a page and then dragged it back to the jar he had selected. He crawled into the jar just as another mosquito tried to land on him.

Lying wrapped up in the newspaper, he tried to get comfortable. The paper had a musty smell, but it seemed to help overcome the jar's strong pickle odor. *This paper should discourage any mosquitoes that are stupid enough to fly into this jar. And paper is good insulation.* Hungry and very tired, he drifted off to sleep.

Before daylight, a violent jostling, accompanied by a thunderous clattering, suddenly awakened Herby. He and the empty glass containers were being toted away.

Chapter 4

Carried
Away

"**I** can't remember these people ever forgetting to set their bins out for pickup," said a voice like thunder to Herby's ears. "Maybe somebody's sick—or just forgot."

Herby pulled the paper from around his head and screamed at the top of his tiny lungs, "Hey! Can't you see me in here? Stop!" But he couldn't be heard above the clatter of the bottles and jars. The bin's contents were dumped into the section of the truck holding glass containers. Herby was still screaming as the driver slammed down the lid.

He bounced along in total darkness for what seemed like hours. *It never occurred to me that I might be carried off like this,* thought Herby. *The driver would have to be a nice guy and do my job for me.*

More containers were piled on top of Herby's jar at each stop. Every time the glass section's lid opened, he yelled, "Hey, mister! Let me out of here!" But his calls were drowned out by the clatter. Bang! clink!

crash! At each stop, the sound of breaking glass caused Herby to grit his teeth and hold his breath.

The truck stopped once more, and he heard voices. Suddenly his jar was falling. Thud!

Herby landed flat on his back. He tried to catch his breath as the jar spun crazily. It finally crashed into some bottles, and a crack streaked across the jar's side.

The jar began moving forward, and Herby got to his knees to peer out. *I'm on a conveyer belt.* Looking around, he recognized the huge room filled with big vats and machinery. His scout troop had visited the recycling plant just last year. As the conveyer belt rounded a turn, its destination came into view. *The glass crusher!* The deafening sound of glass breaking and being crushed filled the air.

He scrambled out of the jar and onto the fast-moving conveyer belt. Wildly looking around for a way to get off, he spied a jacket hanging on a handrail a short distance ahead. The rail was at least a foot from the conveyer belt. It would be a long jump, but Herby had no choice. Mere seconds before he reached the crushing chamber, he leaped for the jacket. His heart skipped a beat when he saw that his outstretched hands were going to miss their target. He was falling!

Whump! Luckily for Herby, he fell into a pocket jutting out from the jacket. While trying to catch his breath, he noticed he was sharing the pocket with a half-eaten sandwich wrapped in a paper napkin. Being terribly hungry and feeling weak, he jerked the napkin away and took a bite of the sandwich. *Mmm, roast beef.*

When he was full, Herby tore off as much of the sandwich as he could carry. He tore the napkin in two and made a headpack. He knew he would have to have his hands free to climb down the jacket. In scouting, he had learned that Native Americans often used headpacks made from animal skins. With the other half of the napkin, he fashioned clothing for himself.

Herby's stomach was full, but he was now very thirsty. Looking along the wall, he spied a large drinking water dispenser. The sight of it made him even thirstier. He crawled out of the pocket and climbed down to hang from the jacket's hem. He dropped a few inches to the floor and then walked to the water bottle. Looking up at it, he thought, *There's no way I can climb up there. Even if I could, I'm too small to push the water dispenser button.* Someone had missed the nearby wastepaper basket, and a wadded paper cup lay next to it. Herby carefully unwadded the cup and, sure enough, there were a few drops of water left in it. He lifted the heavy paper cup to his lips and gulped down the water. As he wiped his mouth with the back of his hand, he thought, *I hope whoever drank from that cup didn't have a cold—or something worse.*

Herby saw several people across the large room, walking back and forth as they worked. He thought about trying to get their attention, but decided it would be too dangerous. They would never be able to hear him in the noisy building. And someone might accidentally step on him. He would just have to leave the building and try to find help.

Walking beneath the conveyer belt, he followed it back to the dock where the recycling truck had dumped its load. He walked out onto the dock and looked up and down the outside of the building. There were several cars and trucks in the large parking lot, but there wasn't a single person in sight.

Herby stepped to the edge of the dock, where several tall weeds grew. He reached out to one and shook it. *This one seems pretty sturdy.* Shielding his eyes from the sun, he scanned the area. Herby wished he had paid more attention when he traveled here with the scouts. The only thing he was sure of was that he lived on the east side of town.

Herby remembered the clock on the wall inside the building showed the time to be past noon. While facing the tall buildings at the center of town, he looked down at his shadow. *My shadow is in front of me, so the sun behind me is in the west. So I'm facing east.* He now knew that to get home he must go toward the center of town and beyond.

He noticed a few rubber bands scattered about on the dock and had an idea. His bare feet felt tender from yesterday's long climb down the trellis and the trek through the flowerbed.

Herby sat down and wrapped each foot with a rubber band. He walked around, adjusting the rubber bands until they felt comfortable on his feet. Thinking he might need spares, he tucked the remaining three rubber bands into his headpack.

Herby returned to the nearby weed and reached out to pull the main stalk close to him. As he climbed onto it, it felt pretty springy, but it held his weight. Cautiously, he climbed down, taking care not to tear his fragile paper clothing. Once on the ground, he couldn't see far at all. He was glad he had plotted which way to go while he was higher up.

He crossed the large parking lot surrounded by a chain-link fence. At the exit, he turned left onto a narrow dirt path that ran between the fence and the street. He walked and walked and walked, passing several warehouses and large fenced lots.

Wham! Something big slammed into a fence and sent Herby running for dear life. He glanced over at a huge guard dog, its teeth bared, growling and barking ferociously.

Herby ran until the barking receded into the distance. His heart pounded, his side ached, and he was out of breath.

When he finally came to a sidewalk, walking was much easier. Suddenly, one of his "shoes" sprang from his foot like a bunch of panicked worms. He sat down and took off his headpack. He took out one of the three rubber bands and wrapped it around his foot.

The sandwich scrap inside the headpack looked tempting. Herby decided he'd better wait to eat it until he found water. Eating it would make him even thirstier than he was already. He put the pack back on his head and wearily started off again.

He crossed one street, a railroad track, and several driveways. Although he looked both ways before crossing, it was still very scary. Knowing it would take him a long time to cross, he ran as fast as his tiny legs would carry him.

With less than a three-inch stride, even after several hours, he hadn't made much progress. Twice, he had to stop to replace the rubber bands on his feet. Since he hadn't found replacements, Herby worried about what he'd do when the ones he was wearing wore out. He was very tired, but knew he must go on.

He also knew he must somehow find water and soon. When he came to another street, he saw trees and bushes on the other side in what appeared to be a park. With renewed energy, Herby looked both ways and then raced across the street.

The deep grass was difficult to trudge through, but after walking on hot cement all afternoon, its coolness felt wonderfully soothing. Herby could hear children laughing in the distance. He made his way toward the sound.

Following the laughter, he could see a family in the distance. A boy and girl were playing chase. A woman sat at a nearby picnic table reading a book.

A huge animal suddenly came bounding toward Herby. It was a playful puppy, but to Herby, it might as well have been a charging elephant!

...Herby looked both ways and then raced across the street.

Chapter 5

Behind
Bars!

H erby made a dash for a nearby trash can. Seeing a
paper sack lying next to it, he dove in headfirst. The
puppy was close behind and grabbed the sack with its
teeth. It began running and playfully shaking the sack
with Herby hanging on inside.

One violent shake of the sack sent Herby flying
through the air. Luckily, the thick, springy grass
cushioned his landing.

Crouching low, he looked around. The puppy, still
shaking the sack, was running toward the children.

Hoping the puppy wouldn't see him, Herby made
his way through the grass toward some nearby bushes.
He crossed through the darkness under them and came
out onto a path. After following the path for some
time, he finally found a drinking fountain. Below it was
a small puddle of water that had spilled over the top.
While wondering if the water was safe to drink, he
spied a few drops on some leaves overhead. Reaching

The puppy was close behind...

up, he gently pulled the plant down until he was able to slurp the drops from its leaves.

Feeling much better, Herby continued down the path. He came upon an old man sitting on a park bench. Herby looked all around, making sure the man didn't have a dog with him.

"Can you help me, mister?"

"Excuse me, sir," he yelled as loudly as he could. "Can you help me, mister?" But the old man was fast asleep and didn't stir. Herby pulled as hard as he could on the man's pant leg, then quickly jumped back.

The old man awoke with such a start that his leg gave a jerk and his hat flew off his head. The hat landed at his feet, just a few inches from where Herby stood. Seeing Herby, the old man's eyes widened, and his mouth dropped open. "Saints be praised! Am I dreamin'?"

Herby shook his head and yelled, "No, mister. I'm real."

Much to Herby's surprise, the old man bent down and snatched him up. He put Herby in the hat and squeezed the brim shut.

"Hey, mister, you don't have to be so rough! Why are you treating me this way?"

The old man didn't answer. He slowly got to his feet.

He chuckled as he began walking down the path. "After all these years, I've finally caught one of ye little rascals."

"What do you mean?" Herby cried out.

"I know all about the likes of ye leprechauns. You're all alike. And a crafty lot, all right."

"I'm not a leprechaun!" Herby protested. "I just accidentally shrank myself."

The old man laughed so hard that he had to stop and wipe his eyes with his free hand.

"Aye, and I'm just a young lad who accidentally

turned himself old overnight."

"Please believe me, mister, I—" began Herby.

"Hush, now!" the old man curtly shot back.
"People will think me daft if they see me talkin' to me
hat. You'll have plenty o' time to entertain me with
your lies when we get home.

It was obvious to Herby that talking was futile, so
he curled up inside the hat. He was exhausted from
the rigors of the day. The hat was comfortable, and the
swaying back and forth as the old man walked lulled
Herby to sleep.

When he finally awoke, Herby thought he was
home in his own bed. He yawned and stretched and
wondered what his mother was fixing for breakfast.
Then he saw bars all around him and quickly sat up.
He was in a cage! An old rusty birdcage. His bed was a
small box, filled with cotton. A handkerchief folded in
two served as sheets. An old worn hand towel carpeted
the floor of the cage.

"Well, I see you're finally stirrin'," said a voice from
across the room. "Would ye be wantin' a bite to eat?"

Herby looked through the bars at the old man.
He was stirring something in a pot atop a small stove.
"Why, yes, sir, I would. I'm awfully hungry." Herby
looked at his hands. They were filthy, along with the
rest of his body,. "But I'm awfully dirty, too. Could I
please have a little warm water and some soap so I can
wash up before I eat?"

The old man shuffled about the room and soon
returned with a small bowl. "Don't try anything funny,

now," he said as he twisted the rusty wire holding the cage door shut. He opened the door and set the bowl of water inside. "Here. Ye for sure could use a bath." Next to the bowl, the man laid a tiny bit of soap and a small piece of sponge.

"Thank you, sir," said Herby as he peeled off the ragged paper napkin. He stepped into the bowl and settled down into the water.

The old man wired the cage door shut and then left the room. He soon returned, opened the cage, and placed two washcloths inside. "Ye can dry on one and wrap up in the other."

"Thank you, sir."

Herby didn't usually relish bathing, but he really needed it, and the warm water felt wonderful.

While Herby bathed and then dried and wrapped himself in one of the washcloths, the old man bustled about the room. He ladled some beans into a bowl and then set it on the table next to Herby's cage. He also set a warm pan of cornbread on the table and a glass of milk.

The old man sat down and peered into the cage at Herby. "See the pincushion? That's your seat. And that spool will be your table. He spooned a little milk into a sewing thimble and handed it to Herby through the bars of the cage. He put two beans, a bit of bacon, and a crumb of cornbread on a measuring teaspoon. "I'll have to open the cage door to pass this to ye. Like I warned ye before, don't try any of your tricks. Ye hear me?"

"Yes, sir. I won't try any tricks."

The old man untwisted the rusty wire and opened the cage door. He handed the spoon to Herby and then quickly shut the door and secured the wire.

The old man began his meal. "I don't remember the last time I had a guest for supper. It's goin' to be nice havin' ye here to take away the lonesomes," he chuckled.

Herby ate every bite of food and drank all his milk. He turned the spoon sideways to pass it and the empty thimble back through the bars. Before clearing away his own dishes, the old man passed a raisin to Herby. "Here's your dessert."

"Thank you. That was sure a good meal."

As Herby munched on the raisin, the old man said, "You're mighty polite for a leprechaun. Mind ye, I've never been acquainted with one before, but I've always heard ye were a grumpy cantankerous lot." The old man watched for a reaction from Herby. But Herby just kept munching on the raisin. "What name are ye called by, leprechaun? And what on earth were ye wearin'? No self respectin' leprechaun should be caught in such shabby attire!"

"My name is Herby, sir."

"Herby!" scoffed the old man. "What kind of a name is that for an Irishman?"

"I'm not from Ireland, sir. As I was trying to tell you earlier—"

"Not from Ireland?" interrupted the old man. "Ye mean to tell me America has little people, too?"

"I don't remember the last time I had a guest for supper."

"I can clear all this up if you'll just let me use your telephone."

"Telephone!" cackled the old man. "Now just what use would I have for a telephone? I know no one to call, and no one cares to call me."

"Do you have today's newspaper? I'm sure it will tell all about my disappearance."

"No. I have no use for a newspaper, either! At least, not since me canary died."

"Then will you please take me to a police station so they can tell my parents I'm all right?" pleaded Herby. "They must be awfully worried."

"There ye go again, ye ungrateful little rascal!" snapped the old man. "Here I give ye a hot bath and a good meal and me reward is a pack o' lies! Don't think I don't know me rights! I'm entitled to one wish from ye, and ye'll not be leavin' me sight till me wish is granted! Understood?"

"No, I don't understand. I don't understand what it is you think I can do for you."

"Ye leprechauns can do just about anything ye set your minds to. Don't ye think I know that? It won't do ye any good to play dumb with me! I've known the legend of the leprechauns since I was a wee lad."

"What would you wish for if by some miracle I *could* grant it?" Herby asked.

"Most people in my position would ask for a huge amount of gold, or stocks, or bonds, or whatever. Me wish is for somethin' much, much more precious." He lowered his head and became silent.

"What, sir? What is so precious to you?"

"Me son," he answered hoarsely. "I want ye to find me son and bring him back to me."

"Where *is* your son?" asked Herby.

"Are ye daft, leprechaun? If I knew that, I'd ask for gold so I could go get him meself!" snapped the old man. "Some years ago, he was accused of a terrible crime. He couldn't prove his innocence, so he fled Ireland and came to the United States. I've had no word of him since."

"Why didn't he call or write to you?"

"He must have been afraid that if he did, the police would be able to trace him and catch him. The scoundrel, who had actually committed the crime, was caught some months later. But not knowin' where me son was, I couldn't let him know he was no longer a fugitive. Now do ye understand why it is so important to me that ye grant me wish? I must find me son!"

Herby nodded "Yes" while thinking, *my own parents must feel the same way about me.* "Where is your wife, sir? She must be awfully worried, too."

"That lovely woman, God rest her soul, has been in heaven these past twelve years. Our son, Grady, Grady O'Sullivan is his name, is our only child."

After a moment of silence, the old man unfastened the door to Herby's cage. "You're goin' to need clothes. I can't expect a leprechaun to do a proper job if he doesn't have proper clothes. Step out here so I can take your measurements. But I'll not be havin' any of your tricks!"

Herby stood very still as the old man measured him. "Just a mite under six inches tall. You're a bit small, even for a leprechaun. But ye appear to be pretty young. I guess ye'll be growin' some. Did ye get enough to eat?"

"Yes, sir. I'm stuffed."

"Good! Now get back inside that cage. And get in bed and cover up with that washcloth so ye don't catch your death. I assume leprechauns catch colds, too. Is that right?"

"I suppose so," answered Herby, shrugging his shoulders.

Herby snuggled into the soft bed-in-a-box and listened as the old man talked. While he was sewing Herby's clothes, the old man spoke of his life as a tailor in Ireland. He came to the United States about four years ago and had used up all his life's savings looking for his son. He now supported himself by doing alterations for a nearby men's clothing store. He had traced his son here to Colorado but hadn't been able to find him.

In Ireland, Grady had been an apprentice to a ship builder. And he had worked for several boat builders in this country. The old man knew he was on the right trail because people who had worked with Grady recognized the photograph the old man carried. But the trail had ended here in the town of Mountainview, and the old man had no idea where to look next. He was still talking as Herby drifted off to sleep.

A shaft of morning light awakened Herby. He saw that his new clothes were lying on the pincushion.

Besides a shirt and pants, the old man had made him underwear, a pair of sturdy boots, and a hat. The hat even had a little feather in it.

The old man was sound asleep, snoring noisily across the room. *He must have worked on these all night,* thought Herby as he quickly dressed in his new clothes. They fit him snugly, and appeared to have been made from a green sock. Herby looked in the mirror the old man had thoughtfully propped up inside the cage. *Not bad. I really could pass for a leprechaun.*

Herby looked across the room to the clock on the wall. It was nearly 6:00 a.m. *If I'm ever going to get home, I've got to get out of here.*

He studied the rusty wire holding the cage door shut. He tried untwisting it, but found he wasn't strong enough. One end of the wire was especially rusted. Herby began bending it back and forth. He worked and worked. After a few minutes, the rusty wire broke in two and fell to the table with a clatter. He winced and glanced across the room. The old man was still fast asleep.

Herby slowly opened the cage door and quietly stepped out. The measuring tape, pencil, and the paper, on which the old man had written Herby's measurements, were still lying there. Herby stood on the paper and shoved the pencil around on it. He hoped the old man would be able to read the crudely scrawled word, "Thanks."

Remembering the knots he had learned in scouting, Herby made a bowline in one end of the

I really could pass for a leprechaun.

measuring tape. He looped it around the stubby pencil and pulled it snug. He put the pencil between the bars of the cage. He turned it sideways to the bars and pulled the measuring tape taut as he backed up to the table's edge.

Rappelling was not new to Herby. He had once rappelled down a large rock face during a scout outing. That training came in handy now as he rappelled down the table leg to the floor.

He ran to the apartment door and squeezed under it. After running a short way down the hall, he came to a staircase. He wondered how he would ever get down it. If he jumped from step to step, by the time he got to the bottom, his feet would be too bruised to walk. If he slid down the steep baseboard edging the stairs, he'd go too fast and crash at the bottom.

To make matters worse, he saw a cat down there. It was napping in the sunshine, which poured through an opening left by a missing windowpane. He would have to move quietly and cautiously to avoid the cat. Suddenly, Herby had an idea. *The pencil! I could slide down the baseboard and use the eraser as a brake.*

He ran back to the apartment door and peeked underneath. The old man was still asleep.

Herby squeezed under the door and ran to the table. He jerked hard on the measuring tape, still dangling off the edge. He jerked and jerked until the pencil turned upright. With one last jerk, the pencil slipped between the cage bars and fell to the floor with a clatter.

Herby's heart seemed to jump to his throat as the old man snorted and sat up in bed.

"Hey! What are ye up to, ye little rascal?"

Herby grabbed the measuring tape and ran for the door, the pencil bouncing along behind. He scooted under the door and quickly pulled the tape and pencil after him.

By the time Herby got to the top of the stairs, he could hear the old man fumbling with the lock. "Come back!" he yelled. "Ye must come back! What about me wish?"

Herby looked down the stairs and saw that the cat had repositioned itself at the very place he had planned to land. *It's either the cat or the old man. I'll just have to brake to a stop before I get to the cat.*

Herby looked down the hallway and saw the old man's door open. *It's now or never,* he thought as he sat down on the steeply sloping baseboard. Dragging the eraser end of the pencil behind him, Herby began sliding fast, but at a controlled speed. Suddenly, the loose end of the measuring tape caught in a crack in a stair step above. Herby was jerked to an abrupt stop. He looked up and saw the old man starting down the stairs. Herby let go of the pencil. He whizzed down to the bottom stair, shot into the air, and landed squarely on top of the napping cat. The cat yowled, and with Herby hanging onto it for dear life, jumped through the opening left by the missing windowpane.

He whizzed down to the bottom stair...

Chapter 6

Kidnapped!

"**S**top! Stop!" Herby yelled at the frightened cat as it dashed along the sidewalk. But the more he yelled, the faster the cat ran. It ran on and on, darting down alleys and through narrow spaces between buildings. As Herby clung to the cat, he saw that he was in a drab and dirty part of town.

In an alley, the still-frightened cat sprang up on a trashcan. From there, it jumped to a high window ledge, where it let out some annoyed yowls. Herby noticed a tear in the window screen. He slid off the cat's back and was able to squeeze through the tear just as the cat swatted a paw at him. *That was close!* thought Herby.

Once inside, Herby looked around the room and saw that he was in the kitchen of a restaurant. He noticed a large sponge lying on a stainless steel counter far below. Taking careful aim, he jumped down to the sponge, bounced, and rolled onto the counter.

Herby heard voices in the adjoining room and a radio playing. As he wondered what to do next, he wasn't paying attention to the news report on the radio until he heard his name spoken. "Herbert Strange has now been missing for thirty-eight hours without so much as a clue to his disappearance. Police Chief Carlson states that the case is highly unusual in that the kidnappers have let so much time elapse without contacting the family with ransom demands."

Herby was straining to hear every word the newsman was saying, when the cat began yowling again. He heard a voice in the next room say, "Hear that? That old alley cat comes around here every day for his breakfast. He's a little early this morning. What did you say? Yeah, that's for sure. That kid's parents would probably pay a lot of dough to get him back. Excuse me, you said your name was Jake? I'll be right back, Jake."

The voice grew progressively louder until a large burly man burst into the kitchen. The words on his greasy apron read, "Bruno's Diner."

The man looked up at the cat in the window. "There you are, Scar! No scraps yet. You're too early. You'll have to settle for a little milk."

The cat continued yowling as the man poured milk into a bowl, opened the back door, and set the bowl in the alley. He watched the cat jump down from the ledge, and then he shut the door.

Now that the cat was quiet, Herby called to the man as loudly as he could. "Sir?"

The man opened the door again and looked up and down the alley. "I must be hearin' things," he said as he shut the door.

"Here I am! Down here!" Herby yelled loudly. The man looked toward the counter, where Herby was waving his arms in the air. A look of disbelief came over the man's face.

From the other room, Jake's voice boomed out, "Hey, Bruno! Is that cat a payin' customer? How 'bout a refill on the coffee?"

The burly man didn't answer. He just stood speechless staring at Herby.

The voice from the other room came nearer. "Hey, Bruno! What's goin' on back here?" Jake appeared at the kitchen door and looked at Bruno. He followed Bruno's stare to the counter and to Herby.

"Do you see what I see?" mumbled Bruno.

"Y-e-a-h. It's one of them little green space creatures."

"Hello! I'm not from outer space," yelled Herby. "I'm from right here in Mountainview. My name is Herbert Strange and —"

"Herbert Strange?" Bruno interrupted. "The kid everyone's lookin' for?"

Herby nodded. "Yes, sir, that's me."

"How come they didn't say how little you was?" asked Bruno. "And why are you so little?"

"I'll tell you all about it. But first, will you please call my home and ask someone to come get me? My number is 787-2643."

"Do you see what I see?"

"Sure thing, little fella," said Bruno as he reached for the phone on the wall.

Jake grabbed Bruno's arm. "Wait! Can't you see what we got here? We got us a potential gold mine."

Bruno looked puzzled.

"Man, you said yourself his parents would pay a lot of dough to get him back," added Jake.

"You mean like a reward?" asked Bruno.

"Yeah, only we'll tell 'em how much the reward's gonna be."

"But that's like asking for a ransom!" Herby protested. "That's what kidnappers do!"

"Yeah," said Jake. "The kid's folks already think he's been kidnapped. They're just waitin' for the kidnappers to tell 'em how much dough they gotta cough up to get him back."

"What you're talkin' about is against the law," Bruno growled. "I don't want no part of it!"

"That's okay with me. Just means I'll get all of it."

"Don't you dare lay a hand on that little fella," said Bruno, as he reached for the wall phone. "I'm callin' his folks right now!"

Suddenly, Jake grabbed a skillet and hit Bruno over the head.

Herby gasped as he watched Bruno drop to the floor.

Herby ran down the counter and tried to jump for the handle of a broom that was propped against the wall. He missed the handle and fell. Just before he hit the floor, Jake scooped him up in his cap.

"See there, ya little shrimp? You almost got yourself killed. Ain't nobody gonna pay money for a dead kid!"

Jake crammed Herby into his shirt pocket. Then he ran into the dining area and grabbed his backpack. He opened the cash register and stole the few bills there. Before he left the diner, Jake turned the "Open" sign around to read "Closed."

Herby bounced around as Jake strode down the street. He finally stuck his head out of Jake's pocket so he could get some fresh air.

Whew! It's been a while since this dude's had a bath!

Still frightened and with a trembling voice, he yelled up to Jake. "Hey, mister! What's your last name?" Herby thought the information would be useful if he ever found a policeman.

"None of your business, shrimp!"

After walking several blocks, Jake came to a highway. Herby finally knew where he was.

He had been through this intersection many times with his parents. Jake began walking backward along the side of the highway, thumbing for a ride.

"Hey, shrimp! When we get a ride, you stay hidden in that pocket. You got it? One peep outta you, and I'll just toss you out a window."

"You can't get away with this!" yelled Herby. "As soon as Bruno wakes up, the police will come looking for you!"

"Don't worry about that," scoffed Jake. "We'll be long gone by then. All I gotta do is make a phone call to your folks when we get to—" Jake stopped himself. "Where we're goin'."

"Where is that?"

"A place where nobody can find us. Now shut up and quit askin' so many questions!"

Many cars went by. Some slowed down, but none stopped. *I sure wouldn't pick up a hitchhiker,* thought Herby, *especially one as grimy as this guy.*

It began to rain. A big raindrop hit Herby on the head and ran down his face. He ducked deeper into Jake's pocket, trying to keep his nose out.

It was raining hard by the time a big semi-truck pulled off the highway in front of them.

"Don't forget, shrimp!" said Jake. "You stay hidden, and you keep quiet or you're out the window!"

Jake opened the truck door and climbed in. Herby heard the door slam. "Where are you headed?" a woman's voice asked.

"Not far, just twenty miles or so down the road."

"Won't be going much farther than that myself," she said. "My husband doesn't want me to pick up strangers, but I just couldn't stand seeing you out there in that cold rain. Why, look at you! You're soaked to the skin!"

"It was awful kind of you to stop, ma'am."

"My name's Kate. What's yours?"

"Uh, John. John Smith," he lied.

"Buckle up, John."

"Ma'am?"

"You forgot to buckle your seat belt."

"Yes, ma'am," said Jake as he buckled up. "Thank you, ma'am,"

Herby listened to Kate and Jake talk about the weather as they rode along. Jake's shirt pocket was wet from the rain, making the stench inside almost unbearable.

"Would you mind if I smoke, ma'am?" Jake asked.

"That's a nasty habit," she said. "It'll put you in an early grave. But if you must, roll down the window enough to let the smoke out. And when you're finished, put your cigarette out in the ashtray. Don't go flipping it out the window, even if it *is* raining."

Jake reached into his other shirt pocket for cigarettes. He lit one with the truck's lighter and inhaled deeply.

The truck's CB radio crackled and a man's voice came over it. "Katydid—calling Katydid. Come in, Kate."

"That's my husband calling," said Kate as she reached for the microphone on the truck's dashboard. "Hi, Gus! This rain is slowing me down some, but I should be home within an hour. Over."

"Drive carefully, sweetheart," answered Gus. "I'll have some hot coffee and a piece of custard pie waiting for you. Out."

Kate placed the mike back in its holder. "That man is a real jewel, he is."

"Sounds real nice," said Jake.

Even with the window partially open, smoke found its way to Herby. He could hardly keep from coughing. He remembered Jake's threat to toss him out the window, and he knew Jake was mean enough to do it. But finally, he could hold it no longer. He coughed and coughed and coughed. Jake thumped the pocket hard, and Herby let out a small, muffled cry.

"What in the *world* do you have in your pocket?" asked Kate.

Jake flipped his cigarette out the window. "Pull over, Kate," he said.

"Sure, John, but why would you want off here? We're in the middle of nowhere, and it's still raining cats and dogs."

Kate pulled the big truck off the highway. The truck braked to a stop with a loud PHSSSH. "Are you sure this is where you want out, John?"

"As a matter of fact," snarled Jake, "I ain't gettin' out here. *You* are."

"*What?*" exclaimed Kate.

Jake grabbed Kate's arm and popped open her seat belt. He reached around her to open her door. "Get out!"

As Kate tried to protest, Jake shoved her out the door and into the pouring rain. He slammed the door shut and locked it.

Jake scooted into position behind the wheel. He had trouble finding the right gear, and the truck growled loudly as he began steering it slowly back onto the highway.

Kate ran alongside, pounding on the truck's door. "Unless you know how to drive a rig like this, you're asking for trouble!" she screamed. "You could kill yourself or someone else!"

Herby's heart beat wildly. He could still hear Kate screaming as the truck pulled away and began picking up speed. Herby stuck his head out of Jake's pocket. "That was a terrible thing you did, leaving that nice lady out in the rain and stealing her truck!"

"It's all your fault, shrimp," snarled Jake. "You shoulda kept quiet like I said. And I shoulda tossed you out the window like I promised. Don't you concern yourself with that mouthy old dame. She can thumb a ride same as I done." Jake laughed a mean little laugh. "Maybe she'll listen to her old man from now on and not pick up strangers."

Herby looked up at Jake. "Do you know how to drive this big truck?" he asked.

"What's to know?" snapped Jake. "We only got a few more miles to go anyway. I know a good place to hide this big baby. And I know someone who'll pay big bucks for her. Gettin' this truck is an extra bonus. This has sure been my lucky day!"

"May I please get out of your pocket?" Herby pleaded.

"Okay. Get over there in Kate's bag. Crawl around and see if you can find any money or jewelry. And don't try anything funny, or I'll swat you like a bug."

Herby climbed down Jake's shirt. He made his way over to Kate's bag and crawled inside. It held balls of yarn and something Kate had been knitting.

"What did you find in there?" Jake asked. "Any valuables?"

"It's just full of knitting stuff," said Herby. He didn't mention the knitting needles he had found in the bag. He might need them later.

Herby looked up at the truck's windshield wipers. It was raining harder than ever. He looked over at Jake. He wondered how anyone could be so mean. Suddenly,

Jake began twisting the steering wheel back and forth. His teeth were clenched, and he looked scared. "Where the devil are the brakes on this stupid rig?" Jake yelled.

Kate's knitting bag slid back and forth on the leather seat as the truck careened around several curves. Herby ducked down in the bag, hoping the balls of yarn would cushion him from the impact he knew was coming. There was a terrible sound of grinding metal as the truck rolled over. The sounds and the tossing about made him sick to his stomach. He wrapped his arms around a yarn ball and held on tightly.

"Where the devil are the brakes on this stupid rig?"

Chapter 7

Escape!

Herby awoke to a dripping sound. It took him a few minutes to figure out where he was. He peeked out of the knitting bag. The bright glare from a window overhead hurt his eyes. The sound he heard was merely the last few drops of rain hitting the window. Sun was peeking out of the clouds, and he could see a rainbow. Herby now realized that the truck was lying on its side.

What's happened to Jake? Where is he? Herby climbed out of the bag and felt a slight movement beneath his feet. He was standing on Jake's shoulder. Jake had not fastened his seat belt and had been tossed around inside the cab. He wound up lying on the passenger-side door. Herby looked up and down Jake's crumpled body. Jake moved a little and moaned.

A loud crackle made Herby nearly jump out of his skin. A man's voice boomed out, "Katydid—Gus calling Katydid. Katy, where are you? You're late, and your coffee's gettin' cold. Over."

It was Gus's voice coming out of the speaker on the truck's dashboard. Herby's eyes followed the dangling spiral cord from there to the microphone lying near Jake's hand.

The voice came back again. "Katydid! Why won't you answer? Gus calling Katydid! Over!"

Herby jumped off Jake's shoulder and hurried to the mike. He tried to push the "talk" button, but couldn't budge it. So he jumped up and came down on the button with both feet. Click! It worked!

Herby yelled into the mike as loudly as he could. "Gus! Listen hard! A bad man stole Kate's truck and it rolled over. He made Kate get out some ways back, but she's not hurt. The bad man also hurt a man in Bruno's Diner. Please send someone to help him. My name is Herby Strange. Please call my family and tell them I'm okay except that I'm—" Herby was going to explain how he'd shrunk. But he was afraid that if he did, Gus wouldn't believe anything else he'd said. "Just get help quick. Okay, Gus?"

Suddenly, Jake's hand jerked and knocked Herby off his feet. He rolled across the passenger-side window, which was still partially open. He caught himself before he rolled right out of it, and wound up within inches of Jake's face. Lying still and barely breathing, he watched Jake. He decided that Jake hadn't heard him talking to Gus on the CB radio. He looked through the windowpane at the ground more than a foot below.

While hanging onto the edge of the windowpane, Herby lowered one leg through the opening. As he pulled his other leg out of the window, he slipped on the wet glass. Instead of landing on his feet, he landed flat on his back in the mud.

With the breath knocked out of him, Herby lay there, unable to move. He studied Jake's face, pressed against the windowpane above him. Jake's eyelids fluttered, and then suddenly opened wide! Herby struggled to catch his breath. He watched helplessly as Jake opened the window and reached out to grab him.

"Hello! Anyone in there?" a man's voice called out nearby. Jake's hand quickly pulled back inside.

Herby sucked air into his lungs and with every ounce of strength he had, got to his feet.

He ran around the cab of the truck toward the sound of the man's voice. But the embankment was very steep, and the rainwater pouring off the highway made climbing difficult.

Herby heard Jake and the man yelling back and forth. He figured Jake was standing up in the sideways truck cab with his head sticking out of the driver-side window.

"Thanks, but I'm fine. I already called for a tow truck on my CB, so help should be here any minute," Jake lied. "There's no need for you to stick around."

"Are you sure?" the man asked.

"Yup, I'm sure."

Oh, no! thought Herby. Breathing hard from the climb, he reached the highway just in time to see the man's car drive away.

Jake pulled himself up through the driver's window. "It won't do you no good to run away, you little brat! You know I'll catch you, so don't even try! There's things out there just waitin' to gobble you up! Your only chance is to stick with me!"

Even before Jake jumped down from the truck, Herby was sliding back down the muddy embankment. On his climb up, he had noticed a culvert running under the highway. He could hide in there.

At the bottom, rainwater was pouring into the culvert. Kerplunk! A large pebble rolled down from above. Herby looked up. Standing on the embankment directly above him was Jake, craning his neck back and forth looking for Herby. Before he could be spotted, Herby slipped into the cold water and let the swift current carry him into the culvert.

It was dark, but Herby could see some stuck tree branches ahead, silhouetted in the light from the other end of the culvert. As the current swiftly carried him to them, he grabbed one and pulled himself up out of the cold water. Climbing high on the branch, he tried to make himself as secure as possible.

He heard another car stop on the highway above, followed by the sound of voices. Then that car sped away too.

Herby sat shivering in the darkness, cold and wet, listening to Jake calling for him and yelling threats. He wondered if Gus had even heard his call. He knew Jake wouldn't call for help. A patrolman is the last person

Jake would want to see. What if Gus hadn't heard him? No one would ever know where he was.

When Herby finally heard sirens approaching, it was like music to his ears! He started climbing down the tree branch, when the light at the entrance to the tunnel was blocked. The dark form entering the culvert was Jake. Herby clung to the branch and stayed still, hoping he wouldn't be noticed. Jake crawled closer and closer, pushing his backpack ahead of him through the water as he came.

Above on the highway, there were sounds of several cars braking and doors slamming. A commanding voice boomed out, "They've got to be around here somewhere. We're looking for a slender, white male with stringy brown hair and an eleven-year-old boy. The boy made the call, but the truck driver said she hadn't seen him. So the kidnapper must have picked the boy up later, probably at a hideout somewhere after he stole the truck.

"Spread out. Let's try to find them before the boy's parents get here!"

Herby's heart leapt to his throat. *My parents! Mom and Dad are on their way here!*

As he crawled deeper into the culvert, Jake's eyes grew accustomed to the darkness. He reached to pull the tree branches out of his way and spotted Herby. "So there you are, you little troublemaker," he whispered.

Just as Jake's hand reached for Herby, a light flashed into the culvert. The same commanding voice

Jake crawled closer and closer...

boomed, "Stop where you are! This is Morgan County Sheriff Jasper Bailey. Do what I say and you won't get hurt. Now, back out of there, and don't try anything funny!"

Even in the dim light, Herby could see the hate in Jake's eyes. "This is all your fault, you little cockroach," Jake rasped. "They ain't gonna find you with me! Or anyplace else for that matter!" Jake snapped off the branch Herby clung to and tossed it ahead as far as he could.

Herby smacked the water hard, and the branch was torn from his grip. He tried to stand up, but the rainwater pouring in had deepened, and he couldn't touch bottom. As he was being swept away, the roar of the water pouring out of the culvert got louder and louder. He thrashed his arms and legs as hard as he could, trying to swim back, but the current was too strong.

Chapter 8

The Long Way Home

Herby felt himself falling and being pounded by the force of the water. His lungs felt like they would burst, but finally he popped to the surface and took a big gulp of air. He was caught in an eddy, swirling around and around. The branch he had been clinging to in the culvert was also caught in the eddy, and he managed to grab it as it bobbed past. Holding on, he kicked and kicked, until he finally broke free of the eddy.

Herby and the branch bobbed down a little cascade, finally reaching a swiftly running creek. Suddenly, he heard a dog barking excitedly. "That's Bozo!" he cried. He felt a surge of hope.

The highway was high above Herby, and he was being carried away. He looked back to see a patrolman climbing down the embankment. Another peered into the end of the culvert Herby had just exited.

"Help! Help!" Herby yelled as the patrolmen climbed back up to the highway. Tears came to his eyes. He sobbed hard as his hopes faded.

Clinging to the branch, Herby floated on and on, bobbing and swirling in the frigid water.

He knew he had to get out of the creek. His teeth were chattering, and he was shaking uncontrollably. He remembered what he learned in scouts about

"Help! Help!"

the danger of hypothermia. *Once the body's core temperature begins to drop, death can occur in a very short time.*

A stand of cattails appeared ahead. Kicking hard, Herby was able to maneuver over to them. He grabbed one and pulled himself to shore. Stumbling out of the water, he dropped exhausted onto a patch of moss. He wanted to stay there and rest, but knew he mustn't. He had to keep moving to stay warm.

Herby forced himself to sit up, and with numb and shaking hands pulled off his boots. After peeling off his wet clothes, he wrung them out and flung them onto a nearby bush. He hadn't eaten all day and knew that his body needed food to warm back up. Looking around, he noticed some grass nearby, heavy with seeds.

Still shivering uncontrollably, Herby struggled to break off a few grass stems and laid them on a large flat rock. He went back to the cattails and found several from last season that were broken and bent almost to the ground. Making several trips, he carried some of the old cattail heads back to the flat rock, where he pounded them with his fists until they were fluffy. Still shivering, he crawled up on the rock and lay down next to the grass stems. The rock, warm from the sun, felt wonderful. He pulled the cattail fluff all around and buried himself in it.

Herby bit into the outer shell of a grass seed, peeled it, and ate the tender morsel inside. After eating several more, his shivering subsided. *If it hadn't been for the stuff I learned in scouts, I'd be a goner by now for sure.* He finally felt the chill leaving, and he drifted off to sleep.

When Herby awoke, he popped his head out of the fluff and wondered how long he had slept. From where the sun was in the sky, he judged it to be early afternoon. He crawled off the rock and brushed off the fluff. *My survival book says the Indians used this stuff for insulation. I can sure see why.*

He gathered his clothes from the bush. They were dry and warm as he put them on. His boots were still a little damp, but he put them on anyway.

Herby picked more grass seeds and bundled them up in a large leaf, which he secured with several long pieces of tough grass.

He scouted the area for a good walking stick and found another to carry the leaf bundle over his shoulder. *It's time to hit the trail,* he thought. *It's going to be a long way home.*

Herby thrashed his way through the tall, thick grass along the creek. Luckily, he soon broke out onto an animal trail. Occasionally the trail branched off, and he took care to stay on the path that followed nearest the creek. He knew the creek ran close to the highway leading home, so was confident about his heading, but had no idea how far he had to go.

After walking for hours, Herby was hungry. He guessed it would be about dinnertime at home. He thought about all the good things his mother might be cooking. He wasn't especially looking forward to his own menu, but he knew he must eat. As he walked, he looked for a nice rock or branch to sit on while he rested and ate.

A dark shadow suddenly flashed across the trail. The stick and leaf bundle were torn from Herby's grip. Instinctively, he dove for cover in the tall grass beside the trail. He looked up to see a hawk flying away, the stick and leaf bundle dangling from its talons.

I see I'm not the only one thinking about a meal.

As shaken as he was, Herby couldn't help but chuckle. *That hawk is sure going to be disappointed when he sees what he caught.*

Keeping a watchful eye for the hawk, Herby began gathering more grass seeds.

He sat under the safety of a bush to eat. Afterward, he was very thirsty.

Scouting had taught him that drinking untreated water could be dangerous. He recalled that once during a hike, his troop came upon an inviting little brook. All the boys were hot and thirsty and wanted to drink from it. The scoutmaster forbade it and told the boys to drink from their canteens instead. Unknown to the scoutmaster, one of the boys disobeyed, saying that his canteen water was too warm. The next day the boy became deathly ill and wound up in the hospital. He almost died. Herby couldn't remember the medical term for the boy's condition, but it was also known as "Beaver Fever."

People can live for weeks without food but only two or three days without water, Herby thought as he made his way through the tall grass along the creek's bank. He knew he had no choice but to drink from the stream.

Back on the trail, Herby studied the plants along the way. Grass seeds tasted okay, but he knew he would soon tire of eating nothing but them. He was pretty sure he could remember what some of the edible plants looked like. Finding one was the trick. He also kept a wary eye for hawks.

Clouds covered the sun, and Herby felt chilled. While studying the clouds, he tripped over something soft and squishy. A ripe squashberry had fallen on the trail. Overhead was a wild squashberry bush, loaded with berries.

One berry seemed as large as a cantaloupe to Herby. Eating just one filled his stomach. He wiped his mouth on his sleeve, and then looked for a large leaf to hold more berries. He wrapped up two, and then found another stick with which to carry the bundle.

Just as Herby slung the bundle over his shoulder, he heard a crashing sound coming toward him through the brush. It sounded big! He ran down the trail as fast as he could. Out of breath, he hid in the tall grass beside the trail. The crashing noise stopped and was replaced by grunting and slurping sounds. Herby peeked out from his hiding place. A huge form was parked in the trail, in the midst of the berry patch. It was a bear! A big black bear was slurping down berries.

He's too busy to notice me, thought Herby. But just in case, Herby kept up a very brisk pace for quite a while.

He's too busy to notice me...

As he traveled along, he noted the different animal tracks on the trail. He had learned to identify those of most animals in the area. To earn his Nature Badge, he had even made plaster casts of some of them. To help keep his mind off his troubles, Herby recited the tracks he had seen on the trail so far. "Chipmunk, rabbit, deer, fox, squirrel, raccoon, birds, mice, and beaver." He also thought about the insects and spiders he encountered and could identify. *What a great opportunity to study these creatures up close. But not too close.*

Because of the gathering clouds, it was getting dark early. Herby knew he should find a safe shelter soon. He thought about what Jake had said— about things out there just waiting to gobble him up. Herby knew

What a great opportunity to study these creatures up close.

77

that nighttime is when most predators are on the prowl.

A cold wind began blowing. It chilled Herby to the bone. He wished he had thought to bring some of the cattail fluff with him. He could have stuffed it in his clothing for insulation against the cold.

He heard splat! And another splat! Splat! A flash of lightning lit up the sky, followed by a deafening clap of thunder.

The lightning flashed again. In that instant, Herby saw a hole underneath a bush beside the trail. He threw his leaf bundle into the hole and dove in after it. Another clap of thunder heralded the roar of hailstones. He watched them ripping leaves off the bush overhead and bouncing off the ground. He shuddered. The hailstones seemed as large as basketballs.

A hailstone bounced into the hole, just missing him. He stepped deeper into the hole. It seemed warmer. He went even deeper, drawn by the increasing warmth. He could see nothing in the total darkness, but figured the warmth had to be coming from some animal. Herby was fearful, but also very chilled, and the warmth drew him deeper and deeper into the hole.

There's something in here, all right! I can smell it.

Chapter 9

Blue Devil Campground

Herby held his hands out in front of him as he stepped cautiously ahead. He touched something warm and soft. It didn't move, so he explored it with his hands. It had long, silky ears. *A rabbit! It's a baby rabbit, not much bigger than I am.* He felt around and counted six babies. They were sound asleep, cuddled next to their mother. Herby snuggled in between two of the babies. The warmth of their bodies soothed his fatigue, and soon Herby too was fast asleep.

Much later, a sudden movement awakened Herby. The den was now dimly lit by the first light of morning, and the baby rabbits were beginning to stir. *I'd better get out of here,* he thought, *before Mama rabbit wakes up.*

Herby stopped at the den's entrance and saw streaks of pink in the dark blue sky. Breathing deeply, he savored the sweet smell of the forest after a rain. He gathered up the sticks and leaf bundle. After shaking

...soon Herby too was fast asleep.

the water off the bundle, he took out one of the berries to eat as he walked.

Hundreds of birds joined in the chorus to greet the new day. Their singing made Herby feel hopeful and glad to be alive. Drops of rain, hanging on the leaves and grass along the trail, sparkled like huge diamonds. He stopped occasionally to admire them and to drink from them.

Many kinds of insects scurried back and forth across the path. Earthworms had surfaced from the saturated soil to escape drowning and were everywhere. Most were longer than Herby was tall and seemed like huge snakes to him. He stopped to admire a spider web, bejeweled with dazzling drops of water. He studied the spider, patiently waiting for its next meal. "Nice job on the web," said Herby.

Farther down the trail, he came upon a chipmunk,

"Nice job on the web," said Herby.

busily stuffing seeds into its cheeks. When it saw Herby, the chipmunk stopped to stare at him.

"Good morning," said Herby. The chipmunk scampered away through the grass.

Herby didn't recognize the plant, but figured that if the chipmunk thought the seeds were okay, they must be safe to eat. He peeled off one seed's thin outer shell and took a bite. *Hey, this is pretty good. It tastes kind of like peanut butter.* He gathered as many of the seeds as his leaf bundle would hold.

Herby walked all morning. The sun was high overhead when he stopped to rest. He peeled and ate several seeds. Then he was thirsty and wished he had found something to carry water in before all the raindrops evaporated. He ate the remaining squashberry. It had dried out a little, but its juice quenched his thirst.

He rested for a while in the shade of a large fern. The sun was high and beating down on the trail when Herby resumed his walk. *It sure gets hot down here. I'm too close to the ground to get any breeze.*

He found a large green leaf and fashioned it into a hat. Wearing it made him feel much cooler. *It's too bad I lost the hat the old man made for me,* he thought. *That poor old man. I wish I could have helped him find his son.*

The trail eventually led Herby to an asphalt road and to an area he recognized. *Blue Devil Campground! This is where we had our last scout campout!*

He excitedly ran down the row of campsites.

There was not a vehicle, tent, nor person in sight. The singing birds were the only sounds he heard.

Where is everyone? he wondered. He finally came to the campground's entrance, where the Campground Road Bridge should be. Only a few boards were left hanging. On the other side of the stream, Herby could see a barricade spanning the road.

Oh, no! No wonder this place is empty. The bridge is washed out!

As he followed the road through the campground, Herby had a disturbing thought. The stream ran into Blue Devil Lake and to get home he would have to go around it. *That lake is huge! It would take me weeks, maybe months, to walk around it.*

Herby noticed an overturned trash can at one of the campsites. Upon investigating, he found several empty soda cans lying about and had an inspiration. *I bet I could make a pontoon boat out of those cans.* He rummaged around inside the trash can and found more. Six! That's perfect! He found several plastic bags. *To make the cans watertight, I can plug up the holes in them with wads of plastic. And this bag with a drawstring would make a perfect sail! I can use the string, too.* His excitement grew as he continued rummaging through the trash.

Herby loaded two cans into a plastic bag, figuring that was as large a load as he could handle. He pulled the bag onto a paper plate, and began dragging the loaded plate. He made two more trips before he had all of his boat-building materials near the lake's edge.

I bet I could make a pontoon boat out of those cans.

Although he was eager to begin work on the boat, he knew he had to find shelter for the night. It must have protection from the weather and predators. While searching for shelter, Herby was also on the lookout for something to eat. He found a patch of dandelions near a large blue spruce tree, its lower branches touching the ground.

Wary of predators, he peered into the darkness beneath the tree's branches as he plucked a dandelion blossom. While munching on the blossom, he ducked under the low branches to investigate. There was a burrow hollowed out at the tree's base. He noticed that the deserted spider web across the entrance was littered with spruce needles. Using a twig, he cleared the sticky web from the entrance and stepped inside. The abandoned burrow did not go back far, but the chamber at its end was big enough for Herby to stand up in.

Back under the tree, he gathered an armload of twigs and carried them back into the chamber. He laid several on the floor going one direction, then another layer going the opposite direction. Then he spread several armloads of spruce needles over the twigs. He laid flat dry leaves over the needles and topped that layer off with a pile of soft dry grass.

The burrow would be safe from the weather, but Herby was still concerned about predators. He studied the burrow's entrance and had an idea. He searched for sturdy sticks that were slightly longer than the entrance was high. One at a time, he pulled each stick upright into the burrow until it stuck fast. *Bars, just like a jail cell*, thought Herby, *except, hopefully, the bad guys will stay on the outside.*

Herby walked back toward the lake. While getting a drink at the water's edge, he noticed a half-buried fishing line. He pulled the long line out of the sand and discovered a fishhook attached to one end. He wound the line around a twig and added it to his boat-building materials. Looking for more line, Herby walked along the shore until he came to a pile of debris that had washed up. It was a fishing line bonanza. Setting to work immediately, Herby wound up each line as he untangled it. When he came to a line that was impossible to untangle, he sawed it in two with the sharp barb of a fishhook.

Herby pulled a smooth stick of driftwood from the debris. *With a fishhook on the end of this, I'd have a perfect boat hook.* Using fishing line, he secured one to the stick. *This might make a good weapon against a predator, too. As the scout motto says, "Be prepared."*

Herby looked toward his big blue spruce tree and saw the last rays of the sun lighting up its top. After adding the bundles of fishing line to his pile of materials, he took a different route back to his new home in order to look for food.

Along the way, he found several edible plants and picked out landmarks to lead him back to them later. He came upon a wild grapevine with little clusters of grapes dangling overhead. Using the hook, he pulled down a cluster and tore it from the vine. He slung the cluster over his shoulder and ate one of the grapes as he walked.

Before ducking beneath the canopy of tree branches, Herby glanced up at the darkening sky. Soft flashes of light lit up the clouds.

Once he was under the tree, Herby couldn't see a thing. He was glad he had prepared his lodging earlier.

Holding one hand out in front of him, he walked ahead until he touched the tree's trunk. Walking sideways, he felt his way to the burrow's entrance. After laying down his pole and cluster of grapes, he squeezed through a gap he had left in the barricade. He found the stick he had left nearby and pulled it into place to close the gap.

Feeling around in the dark, Herby found his bed and then burrowed into the soft grass. He lay awake for quite a while, planning the building of the boat.

Aunt Bert's husband, Bud, owned a little sailboat and had often taken Herby sailing. He also helped Herby and several other scouts qualify for their Small Boat Sailing Badges by giving them sailing instructions on this very lake.

Herby pondered his past boating experience until the crickets finally lulled him to sleep. In his dreams, he was an explorer, sailing uncharted seas.

Thump! Herby was awakened early the next morning from a deep sleep. Thump—Thump.

He quietly made his way to the barricade and peeked between the sticks. Thump.

Something landed nearby. Herby pulled out one of the sticks and squeezed through the barricade.

After picking up his weapon, the fishhook pole, he cautiously stepped away from the burrow. A spruce cone thumped to the ground, barely missing him. A loud chattering came from high in the tree. Herby looked up to see a gray squirrel glaring down at him and flicking its tail.

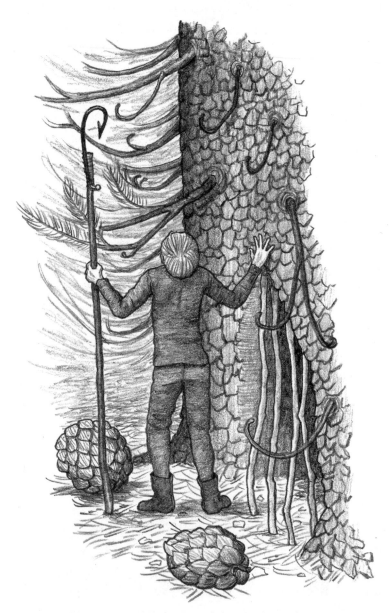

A loud chattering came from high in the tree.

"Okay, okay!" yelled Herby. "You don't have to be so rude! I'll be leaving soon!"

As Herby stood looking up at the squirrel, he felt something touch his leg. He looked down. "Yikes!" With his foot, he lifted the huge wiggling ant and slung it away from him. Then he noticed the ant wasn't alone. Hordes of them were crawling on and around his grapes. With the fishhook pole, he pulled the cluster of grapes away from the burrow. He dragged it into the woods, far from the spruce tree. The ants followed.

Leaving the grapes to the ants, Herby retraced his steps to the grapevine. He tore off a small cluster and ate one of the grapes on his way to the lakeshore. Hoping to discourage more ants, he laid the cluster in the sand at the lake's edge.

Herby pulled some materials from his pile and went right to work. He stretched out a plastic bag and used a fishhook to cut it into strips several inches wide. After tying a strip tightly over and over, he had a fair-sized lump of plastic. He pushed the lump into the pour hole of one of the soda cans. Using a stick, he poked and prodded the lump until it was wedged snugly in the hole. After all six cans were made watertight, he pressed their ends together and made two rows of three cans each.

Making several trips to the debris pile, Herby gathered driftwood sticks for the boat's frame. He also found a sturdy oblong piece of driftwood with a knothole in it. *This is great! I can anchor the boat's mast in the hole.* He chose a thin flattened piece of driftwood to serve as both a rudder and tiller to steer the boat. Something black was sticking out of the pile, and Herby climbed over to investigate. It turned out to be a piece of rubber matting, and he pulled it free of the packed mud and sand.

By the time he had dragged all his newly-found materials back to his workplace, the sun was beating down. Herby was glad hc would be working in the shade of a large driftwood log.

The first job was to lay out the sticks for the frame of the boat's deck. Measuring an equal distance between them, he laid out the four longest sticks. Three shorter sticks were laid across them, one at either end and one in the middle. During a past scouting campout, the boys had been taught lashing techniques. Now that experience came in very handy as Herby lashed the sticks together with fishing line.

Wide strips of plastic were used to tie the cans together end-to-end. By the time Herby had finished that job, he was exhausted and very hungry. He had stopped working several times to get a drink of water from the lake, but had been so busy that he forgot to eat. The shadows were already beginning to lengthen.

Herby looked at the palms of his hands. They were bright red and sore. *I better not tie any more knots today. I can't afford to get blisters. I need to gather food for the trip anyway.*

Looking for the grapes he had left there earlier, Herby walked back and forth along the lake's edge.

They were gone. Deciding a wave must have carried them away, he picked up his fishhook pole and started for the woods.

While searching for something to eat, Herby came upon a plantain plant. He took a bite out of one of the leaves. It didn't taste very good, but he ate it anyway. His sore hands reminded him of something he had read from his book on wilderness survival: *When crushed and applied to swellings, bruises, and wounds, plantain leaves are very healing.* He tore several more big leaves from the plant.

Herby gathered seeds from several different kinds of grasses. He ate some and put the rest in one of the plantain leaves to take on the voyage. He figured that when the seeds were all gone, he could eat the package too. He also picked a few berries to take along.

Leaving his leaf packages in a pile, Herby headed back to the lake for one last drink of water before bedtime. On the way, he stopped at his workplace to assess the work left to do on his boat. Struggling with the heavy frame, he lifted up one side and leaned it against one row of cans. He wiped the sweat from his brow and wondered how he was going to lift the heavy frame up on the cans. Hopefully, he could figure that out tomorrow.

At the lake, Herby drank his fill, and then washed his hands and face as best he could. On returning to his leaf packages, he crested a little hill of sand and saw a large pinion jay pecking away at one of them.

Herby broke out running. "Hey! Get away from there!" he yelled.

The bird lifted off the ground, taking the package and its contents with him. He landed on a nearby picnic table, where he continued pecking away at the package.

"You darned lazy camp robber!"

The bird seemed unconcerned by Herby's outcry.

"Go find your own food!"

Grumbling, Herby loaded up the rest of his packages. Even without the stolen package, Herby had quite a load to carry to his burrow.

When he reached the spruce tree, Herby stuck the packages in some low hanging branches where ants couldn't get to them. He squeezed through the gap in the barricade and then secured it with the stick.

In the fading light, Herby began crushing a plantain leaf, working it between his hands.

He thought he heard something and stopped to listen. Hearing nothing more, he resumed treating his sore hands. He stopped suddenly. *There it is again!* A rustling sound was coming from his bed of spruce needles, leaves and grass. *Oh, no! I know a big snake couldn't get in here, but even baby rattlesnakes are deadly poisonous!*

Chapter 10

Herby Builds His Boat

Herby dropped the plantain leaf and backed slowly toward the barricade. His eyes were now accustomed to the dim light, and he watched his bed intently as he opened the gap and bent down to pick up his fishhook pole. Suddenly, a head with big ears and beady eyes popped out of the grassy bed cover.

"It's just a deer mouse!" cried Herby. Relieved, he said to the mouse. "You'll have to leave. That's *my* bed!"

The surprised mouse scampered past Herby and out of the burrow. Herby replaced the stick in the barricade.

He retrieved the plantain leaf and tore it into strips to wrap around his hands. Kneeling beside his bed, he said, "Hello, God, it's me again, Herby Strange. Thank you for helping me find food and a safe place to sleep. I hope you'll be with me as I sail across the lake. In case I don't make it, is there some way you can let my family know how much I love them? Amen."

"It's just a deer mouse!"

There was a big lump in Herby's throat as he crawled into bed. He pictured his mother crying and his father pacing the floor. He had already seen his Aunt

Bert crying. He was lonesome for his family, and his friends, and Bozo. He even missed his bratty little sister, Suzanne. *What if I never see them again?* He suddenly erupted into tears and sobs. He cried and cried until his exhaustion took over, and he fell fast asleep.

Dew was heavy on the grass and leaves when Herby left his shelter the next morning.

The sky was just beginning to lighten, and only a few birds were singing. Even the cranky gray squirrel wasn't up yet. Herby drank his fill of dewdrops before loading up with his leaf packages and fishhook pole.

As he walked toward the lake, it became harder and harder for Herby to see. *I couldn't have sailed this morning, even if the boat had been ready*, thought Herby, *not in this fog. I'll be lucky if I can just find the boat.*

A short distance ahead, something white fluttered. It acted just like a ghost. Herby didn't believe in ghosts, but then again he might if he ever actually saw one. With his heart beating rapidly, he cautiously approached the thing. He laughed aloud when he saw what it was. A plastic bag was caught on a tall weed and fluttering in the breeze. "I'm going to put you to work, ghost," he said as he pulled the bag down and put his packages inside. Dragging the load was much easier than carrying it, and the plastic bag might be needed later.

Herby found his own footprints, coming from the opposite direction. Since he couldn't see very far ahead in the fog, he followed them, knowing they would lead him to the lake. Sometimes, they were hard to find among the many animal tracks.

The thick fog began to lift, and Herby could see the large driftwood log ahead. There was something about the log that he hadn't noticed before. A broken-off stub of a branch was directly over the boat. *That's how I'll lift the frame up on the cans!*

Herby hung the plastic bag on another stub of the log, where he could keep an eye on it.

After unfolding the bag that would be the sail, he pulled out the drawstring. He tied one end of the string to the deck frame and the other to a lead sinker. Twirling the cord around several times, he tossed the sinker up toward the branch's stub. It missed, and he jumped back as the sinker crashed to the ground. After Herby tried several more times, the sinker finally went over the stub, taking the string with it.

"Yeah!" yelled Herby.

When he pulled on the string, the deck frame lifted off the ground. "It's working!" he cried. He tied the string off several times and maneuvered the frame around until it was in place.

Using strips of plastic and fishing line, he lashed the frame securely to both rows of cans. Next, he attached the piece of driftwood that would hold the mast. He then lashed sticks across the frame to make the deck. He took special care attaching the driftwood, which was both the rudder and tiller. To steer the boat, it had to be moveable, yet sturdy.

Climbing on and off the boat became tiring. Herby stopped to make a rope ladder, using a piece of twine. All boats should have a safety ladder anyway.

"It's working!"

A dark form suddenly appeared a few feet away and startled Herby. A deer had come so quietly that Herby hadn't heard her approach. Staying very still, Herby watched as the doe lowered her head to drink from the lake. A shy, little fawn came up beside her to do the same. After they drank their fill, the two left as quietly as they had come.

It was well past noon by the time Herby stopped to rest and eat. The fog was long gone, and it turned out to be a beautiful day.

It looks like I won't get off today after all. And I've been working as fast as I can.

He looked at the palms of his hands.

I forgot about how sore they were yesterday. That plantain leaf sure did the trick. I'll give my hands another treatment when I finish work today.

Herby stepped to the lake's edge to get a drink. A red plastic bottle cap bobbed around in the water, and Herby waded out to it. He scooped water into the cap, took a big drink, and then carried the cap to shore.

Needing a straight green stick to use for the mast and another for the boom, Herby set off for the woods. He couldn't risk using driftwood, which might snap when stressed by the wind in the sail. He had his pick among several twigs that a squirrel had dropped while making a nest. After stripping them of leaves and bark, he made two trips dragging the sticks to his boat.

Herby smoothed the plastic bag out on the ground, and using a fishhook, cut out the triangular-shaped sail. He threaded the part that held the drawstring over the mast, and then lashed the bottom of the sail to the boom. He tied a long piece of twine to the top of the sail. Known as a halyard, it would raise and lower the sail. Near the mast's top, he attached the four lengths of fishing line that, when attached to the deck, would steady the mast.

I almost forgot! I need a wind indicator so I can tell which way the wind is blowing.

There were plenty of duck feathers lying about, and he picked a nice one to tie to the very tip of the mast. He then tied the same string to the mast that he had used to raise the deck.

Luckily, the string dropped over the branch stub at the first toss of the lead sinker. With Herby pulling hard on the string, the mast lifted off the ground. As with the frame, he tied off several times and maneuvered the mast around until it was firmly in place. After removing the string from the mast, he tied each of the four lines in place at the deck's edges. Using a pebble, Herby hammered a fishhook into the base of the mast, where he would tie off the halyard.

He pulled the halyard and up went the sail. After tying it off, Herby jumped down from the boat and backed away to admire his work. Pretending to be a pirate, Herby put his hands on his hips and loudly said, "By gum, she looks pretty seaworthy, she does!" He called to some gulls floating a short distance away. "Avast ye Mateys! By what name shall we call her?"

Herby had been so engrossed in his work he hadn't noticed the dark clouds gathering above. A strong wind came up, and the sail began swinging back and forth. Herby quickly climbed aboard and hauled it down. He wrapped it around the boom as best he could and then tied the end of the boom to the deck. The feather atop the mast was blowing straight out.

There were whitecaps on the lake, and waves began sloshing up on the shore. A storm was brewing.

Herby thought as he tied the boat to the log, *If the lake rises during the night, I wouldn't want her to leave without me.*

"Splat," sounded the first raindrop. Herby grabbed the remains of the plastic bag and wrapped it around himself. Making several trips, he dragged all his materials to higher ground. He picked up his fishhook pole and plastic bottle cap and ran toward the shelter of his spruce tree. On the way, he stopped long enough to pick a few seeds and a berry and put them in the bottle cap. He stopped again to tear off a plantain leaf.

Standing in the dry shelter of the spruce tree's branches, Herby ate his supper while watching the rain falling hard on the ground. When he finished eating, he set the bottle cap out in the rain.

The burrow was almost completely dark when he entered. He poked around in his bed with the fishhook pole before securing the barricade. *If all goes well, after tonight the critters can have this bed.*

Herby took off his wet boots, crawled into bed, and wrapped his sore hands with the plantain leaf. He began saying his prayers, but was so tired that he drifted off to sleep before he could finish.

Boom! A loud crash of thunder awakened Herby. He lay in bed listening. He knew lightning was usually drawn to the tallest tree in an area. He knew his tree was taller than most and hoped it was shorter than some.

Chapter 11

Can-do

Herby had planned to get up before daybreak to get an early start, but he'd had a hard time getting back to sleep after the thunderstorm. When he finally awoke, the sun was already up. He hurriedly pulled on his boots and then slipped through the barricade. The gray squirrel was raising a ruckus when Herby said goodbye to his home under the big spruce tree.

He drank the rainwater from the bottle cap he'd left out, and then used it to hold what food he gathered on the way to the lake. He plucked a clover blossom, shook the water out of it, and ate it as he walked. *What shall I call my boat,* he wondered. *All boats should have a name.*

As he approached the lake, Herby saw a flurry of activity around the driftwood log where his boat was tied. The lake had risen during the night, and the boat was floating in a few inches of water. Several mallard ducks were standing on the log and more were splashing around it. They seemed very curious about Herby's boat.

"Well, what do you ducks think of my boat?" yelled Herby. "Do you think she can do it?" *Can-do! That's her name!* "Can-do can do it!" he yelled.

The ducks stopped their splashing and stared at Herby. He sloshed through the water toward his boat, and they all took off in a loud, quacking flurry of feathers. Herby ducked as one barely missed him.

Herby checked *Can-do* over. The little boat seemed to have weathered the storm without any damage. She was not listing at all, so he knew her soda-can pontoons had remained watertight. *That rain sure did me a big favor. Now I won't have to drag the boat to the water.*

Herby waded back to shore and to his materials stash.

He spread out a piece of plastic on which he laid a flat piece of wood. Next, he piled the three strips of rubber matting and rolls of fishing line. He dragged the loaded plastic to the water, and then floated the load to the boat. After pulling the rubber strips up on the boat and laying them out, he lashed them to the sticks of the deck.

After a couple of hours of hard work, Herby wiped his brow. "That's it, *Can-do*, you're ready to sail."

It had been a calm morning so far, and Herby had been concerned about the lack of wind. He felt a slight breeze and looked up at the feather atop the mast. It was beginning to flutter a little.

In a gruff voice, he said aloud as he climbed off the boat, "Now, Matey, I'll load me gear and cast off." Pretending to be an old sailor made him feel less apprehensive about the dangerous journey ahead.

Herby floated the piece of wood back and forth to load the supplies he had gathered for the trip—plastic bags, fishing line and string, the sinker that would be his anchor, a plastic knife and two plastic spoons, two fishhooks wrapped in plastic bag scraps, the bottle cap, and the fishhook pole.

After the supplies were loaded, Herby tied them all down. With the pole, Herby retrieved the food stash in the plastic bag he'd left hanging on the log. After rolling up the bag and tying it down, he looked around and said, "By golly, I think I've got everything."

Herby squinted his eyes and looked out on Blue Devil Lake. On past camping trips, he had looked across it from almost this very spot. Before, he had been able to see land on the horizon. Because of his smallness, all he could see now was an endless expanse of water.

He climbed down the rope ladder hanging from Can-do's stern and untied the line attached to the log. Rolling up the line as he waded back to the boat, he thought, *Uncle Bud taught us to always keep the lines rolled up neatly when not in use.* With a great heave, he tossed the roll onto the deck.

The motion thrust the boat away from him. *Oh, no!* thought Herby as he dove into the icy water. He swam and swam as *Can-do* floated farther and farther away from shore. With what seemed like his last breath, Herby finally reached her. He grasped one of the lines that held the deck frame to the cans. He pulled himself around to the stern of the boat and grabbed the rope ladder dragging in the water.

Shaking from exertion, Herby pulled himself aboard. By now, he was nearly thirty feet from shore. As he lay panting on the deck, he thought, *that was way too close! I should have remembered to hang onto the line until I was aboard.*

Herby unsteadily got to his feet and pulled the rope ladder aboard. He looked up at the feather atop the mast to see what direction the wind was blowing.

With the tiller, he turned *Can-do* to face the wind. After tying the tiller in place, Herby raised the sail and tied off the halyard. While hanging onto the boom to keep the sail from swinging back and forth, he set the tiller for the direction he wanted to go. He then set the sail for its best angle to the wind. It filled with wind, and *Can-do* seemed to lift off the water as she went skimming along.

"Yippee! I did it! This mighty boat really moves!"

It wasn't until he had tied both the boom and the tiller in place that Herby noticed his teeth were chattering. He peeled off his wet clothes and wrung them out. After running a line through both sleeves and pant legs, he then tied the line to the end of the boom where his clothes snapped and flapped in the wind.

While waiting for his clothes to dry, Herby wrapped up in a piece of plastic bag and sat huddled on the deck. *I forgot how much colder it is when you're out on the water.*

The wind and sun dried his clothes in no time. *They needed washing anyway,* Herby thought as he dressed. *Now I'd better find something to cover my head before this sun bakes my brain.*

Herby pulled one of the large plantain leaves from his stash. After tearing it in two, he chewed around the edges of the leaf to round it out. He ran a string through two holes he had poked in it and then tied the leaf to his head.

As *Can-do* sailed along, Herby often looked back at the shore and his tall spruce tree. His destination was a lakeside resort and marina directly south across the lake. But he had no other landmarks than the ones he was leaving behind. When he could no longer see them, he could only guess at the proper direction to steer. Luckily, he had a steady wind from the northwest.

Herby remembered that in almost the exact center of the lake, there was a small island covered by tall pine trees. If he could spot it, he thought he should spend the night there. But then, the island was farther to the west and out of the way.

"What do you think, *Can-do?* The wind is perfect now, and it may not be so perfect tomorrow. Should we head for the island or straight away for the marina?"

Herby hesitated, as if listening for an answer. "You're right, *Can-do*! Lights from the marina will guide us in the dark." Herby knew that if he could at

Luckily, he had a steady wind from the northwest.

least see the tips of the tall trees on the island, it would help him know where he was on the lake.

As he sailed, Herby constantly scanned the horizon. He searched for the island, but the sight he most wanted to see was the tall microwave tower near the resort area across the lake.

Herby had no way of knowing how fast *Can-do* was traveling, but he finally lost sight of the shore behind him. He didn't know if it would be days or hours before he would see any other landmarks. "I hope you know where you're going, *Can-do*, because without a compass or landmarks, I don't even know for sure if we're going in the right direction."

When he wasn't tacking or adjusting the sail, Herby busied himself by making a bucket from the plastic bottle cap. Using a fishhook, he drilled two holes near its rim and then made a handle for it from fishing line. So he wouldn't accidentally drop the bucket overboard while getting water, he tied a string to the handle and the opposite end to the boat. That gave him the idea to tie a string around his waist with the other end tied to the mast.

While filling his new bucket with drinking water, he spotted a few treetops on the horizon. "Look there, *Can-do*, on your starboard side. It's the island. I'd say we're pretty much on course and already halfway across the lake. At this rate, we should see the tower on the far shore before dark—as long as the wind doesn't die."

Herby's stomach growled and reminded him that it was well past noon. He ate some seeds from his food stash and had a berry for dessert, all the while scanning the horizon for the tower. He also often checked the island as it gradually receded into the distance.

In late afternoon, the wind shifted and the sail began flapping wildly. Herby glanced up at the feather atop the mast. "Oh, no, *Can-do*! The wind is coming directly out of the south, and we need to go south!" Not only had the wind changed direction, but it had become much stronger.

Herby quickly untied the halyard and pulled down the sail before it could be ripped to shreds.

Even without the sail, *Can-do* was pushed rapidly along by the wind. To keep from being blown clear back across the lake, Herby turned *Can-do* around and steered back toward the little island.

Huge waves crashed over *Can-do*'s deck. Soaking wet and shivering, Herby grabbed at a large food stash as it slid out of its ties and over the side. "It's a good thing I tied myself to the mast, *Can-do*, or I'd have gone over too."

Herby struggled with the tiller to stay on course and felt as if he were riding a roller coaster. "Hang in there, *Can-do*," he screamed.

As the little boat approached the island's shore, Herby grabbed his fishhook pole. Hanging tightly onto the line connecting him to the mast, he stood ready to push away from any rocks or debris he might encounter.

Luckily, *Can-do* was blown into a clump of reeds. Herby shoved the pole to the bottom to see how deep the water was. *Just about waist deep.* With the tie-up line in hand, he hopped off the side of the boat. "Huff!" His breath squeezed out and pain grabbed him around his waist. He hung off the side of the boat just above the water. *Oh, no! I forgot to untie myself.*

With much thrashing about, he was finally able to clamber aboard *Can-do* and slip out of the line. He looked up at the dark sky. It had become threatening, and the wind was blowing even stronger. With the tie-up line in hand, he hopped into the water to pull *Can-do* closer to shore. "Come on, *Can-do*, these reeds will give you some protection from the weather."

BAM! A bolt of lightning hit nearby.

Herby wrapped the line around several reeds and tied it fast. Grabbing his fishhook pole and a roll of plastic, he waded to shore to look for shelter.

It was evident that campers and picnickers frequented the island. Herby found several rock fire rings and a great amount of trash littered about. *How gross! If people can bring their stuff here, why can't they take their trash back when they leave?* He angrily kicked a bottle cap and sent it flying.

Splat. Splat. Raindrops began to fall. Herby ran from one tree to another, looking for a burrow or anywhere he could take shelter. A large tin can rolled past him in the wind, and he ran to stop it. Peering inside, he was surprised at how clean it was. To secure it, Herby shoved the can under the branches of a low bush and then draped the plastic over its open end. As he pulled back the plastic to crawl inside the can, he saw movement out of the corner of his eye. It was a brightly colored scarf caught on the bark of a nearby tree. He ran to retrieve it before it blew away.

He pulled the scarf from the tree trunk. It was silky and wonderfully soft, carrying the sweet scent of perfume. As he held it next to his face, a wave of loneliness swept over him. It reminded Herby of his mother and somehow made him feel safe. A few large raindrops reminded him to take cover.

He ran back to the can, pulled back the plastic, and stuffed the scarf inside. By the time he had crawled inside the can and snuggled up in the scarf, it was almost completely dark. Another clap of thunder brought the pouring rain. Occasional flashes of lightning shone through the plastic. Knowing that bodies of water draw lightning, Herby was glad he was not out on the lake. Through the rhythmic sound of raindrops beating on the can, he drifted off to sleep.

When Herby pulled back the plastic the next morning, the birds were singing and the sun was shining brightly. He bundled the scarf and plastic under his arm and headed back to *Can-do*. Along the shore, he found some young cattail shoots and broke off a couple. He would eat them for breakfast once he was on his way.

Can-do had weathered the storm just fine. Herby waded out to her, holding the bundled scarf and plastic above his head. The lake had risen during the night, and his feet soon lost contact with the bottom. He swam with one arm while dragging the bundle behind him.

After climbing aboard, Herby looked at the feather atop the mast to check the direction of the wind. "It looks good, Can-do," he said as he pulled up the sinker, which he used as an anchor. "Time to be on our way."

To get the boat moving, Herby used the fishhook pole to push against the lake bottom. He ran back and forth on deck, pushing with the pole in back and pulling through the reeds up forward.

Once he was out of the reeds, Herby used the plastic knife as an oar. He paddled on one side of Can-do and then the other until he was far enough away from shore to raise the sail. He checked the position of the sun to determine his direction, and he was on his way again.

The air on the lake was chilly. Herby was glad when his clothes were dry and he could put them back on. The silk scarf was dry too, and he stashed it in a safe place on the deck. Can-do was making good time and sailing smoothly when there was a thumping sound against her port side. Then there was another thump against her starboard side. Herby peered over the deck into the water. Can-do was right in the middle of a school of big carp. Herby worried that they might tip the little boat over.

"Shoo! Get away from here!" yelled Herby to no avail. The fish thumped and banged against Can-do for some distance, and then suddenly they were gone. "Good riddance!" yelled Herby.

While scanning the horizon, he saw a small boat in the distance. "Look, Can-do," Herby cried. "There's

"Shoo! Get away from here!"

help!" He set sail and changed course to head toward the boat. As he got closer, he saw two men fishing out of it.

"Ahoy, there!" yelled Herby. "Look over here!" He didn't know what the word meant, but he remembered that in the movies, sailors seemed to yell "ahoy" a lot.

"They see us, *Can-do*! They're reeling in their lines so we won't get tangled up in them." Herby waved vigorously. He was about to yell "ahoy" again, when the motorboat's engine came to life with a roar. He watched sadly as the boat sped off into the distance. *I guess they didn't see us after all.*

Can-do suddenly began rocking violently. Herby wrapped his arms around the mast and hung on for dear life. Water splashed over him. He saw his fishhook pole slide over the side. He was glad the rest of his supplies were tied down. *Can-do* had been caught in the motorboat's wake. The little boat bounced around for quite awhile before settling down.

Herby readjusted the sail to get back on course and tied the rudder in place while he ate lunch. Although the wind was uncomfortably cool, it had kept him on a steady course all morning. His clothes were still a little damp, so he stretched out on the deck to keep out of the wind. The warmth of the sun and *Can-do*'s gentle rocking soon lulled him to sleep.

When Herby awoke, he jumped to his feet, furious with himself. *I shouldn't have gone to sleep! I wonder if we're still on course.* He peered around the sail. There it was! The tower! "We're almost there, *Can-do*!"

As he got closer, Herby began looking for a good landing spot. He studied the buildings along the shore. One had a large sign that read "Wayside Marina." *That's where Uncle Bud keeps his sailboat,* Herby recalled. Another sign read "Cozy Inn—Cabins for Rent." One building had quite a few boats on trailers parked around it. Its sign read "Grady O'Sullivan's Boat & Engine Repair." *Grady O'Sullivan. That name sounds familiar.* After a few seconds, Herby remembered. *The old man's son! I'll bet that's him.*

Herby felt excited at the prospect of reuniting the two. *Maybe I'd make a good leprechaun after all.* He steered directly toward the boat repair dock. He could hardly wait to get to shore and find the son. But as he got closer, the dock seemed to be slipping sideways away from him. "We need to tack again, *Can-do*."

He untied the boom and tried to turn *Can-do*. She wouldn't turn. He lowered the sail and checked the rudder. There was no debris hung up on it, and it was able to turn just fine. Yet no matter which way he set the sail or tried to steer, *Can-do* would not respond. Not only that, the boat was moving directly into the wind. *This can't be!*

There could be only one explanation. *Can-do* was caught in a strong current.

Oh, no! I forgot all about the spillway over the dam! The recent rains had raised the level of the lake considerably. The excess water created a strong current as it moved toward the spillway. Herby grabbed the plastic knife and paddled frantically. No matter how hard he paddled, *Can-do* sped faster and faster in the opposite direction.

Just as the little boat slid over the spillway's rim, Herby threw himself on deck and wrapped his arms around the base of the mast. *Can-do* twisted and turned dizzily as she slid down the steep cement slope. The trip seemed to take forever as the roar of the water at the bottom got louder and louder. *Goodbye, world,* thought Herby, as his eyes squeezed shut.

Chapter 12

Disaster!

C rash! *Can-do* exploded into a hundred pieces as
she hit a rampage of water. Herby opened his eyes.
Millions of turquoise bubbles danced around him.
A kaleidoscope of colors swept before him. *So this is
heaven. How beautiful it is.* He then realized that he
was looking through the silk scarf, billowing around
him underwater. The water tumbled Herby over and
over, wrapping the scarf around him.

He finally surfaced and took a big gulp of air. He
grabbed at a couple of sticks as they slid by. They were
still lashed together. The water quickly carried him
downstream.

Poor Can-do, thought Herby as he clung to what
was left of her. Looking back, he saw several cans from
her pontoons bouncing around in the turbulence. He
felt sad, as if he had just lost a good friend. He looked
ahead at the white water before him. *Oh, no! Here I go
again!*

A kaleidoscope of colors swept before him.

The river below the dam was usually fairly tame, but water spilling over had turned it into a raging torrent. The landscape sped by as the river carried Herby farther and farther downstream. *At least I'm going in the direction of home*, he thought.

A bridge lay ahead, and on it several children were playing and throwing stones in the water. When Herby was directly under them, they pointed toward him and laughed. A stone hit the scarf flowing behind him, and he was jerked under water, nearly losing his grip on the sticks.

Coughing up water as he passed under the bridge, he saw that the children had crossed to the other side. They were watching for their target, the brightly colored scarf, to reappear. One girl was about to throw a stone when Herby waved and yelled, "Stop! Please help me!"

But the children could not hear him above the roar of the river. He heard one boy cry out, "Did you see that? What *was* that?"

Herby looked back to see the children running toward the end of the bridge to investigate. But he was too far downstream by the time they reached the riverbank.

As he was carried swiftly along, he shivered and knew he had to get out of the cold water soon. Ahead, a large pine tree had fallen from its hold on the riverbank and was lying partially in the water. As Herby went under the tree, he grabbed at a branch. He missed, but was suddenly jerked to a stop. The scarf had caught on the branch.

Herby used the scarf to pull himself back to the branch, where he climbed out of the water. After tearing the scarf free from the branch, he tied it tightly around his waist.

He walked up the sloping tree trunk to where it ended in a mass of branching roots. Looking between two large roots, he saw a huge gaping hole in the riverbank below. The river had eroded the bank right up to where the big tree once stood. The trip to the ground was going to be treacherous. Climbing down one of the muddy, slippery roots was Herby's only choice.

Very cautiously, he began his descent. He stopped often to wipe his muddy hands on the scarf. About halfway to the ground, Herby looked down and froze. From above, he had not seen that the root he had chosen was one of several that broke off when the tree fell. There was nothing but a foot or more of air between him and the riverbank. He tried reaching over to an unbroken root, but it was too far away. He tried climbing back up, but the root was too slippery.

His only option was to jump and hope that the mud was still soft. Herby carefully studied the narrow strip of riverbank where he would have to land. If he landed too far to the left, he'd end up in the big hole. Too far right would put him right back in the river.

Taking a deep breath, Herby pushed off from the root. He felt his foot slip, and he lost his balance. He landed on the riverbank with a thud, and a sharp pain shot through his left ankle. "Now I've done it!" he cried. Lying on his back in the mud, Herby gritted his

teeth against the throbbing pain. His body began
to shake.

Fighting against the pain, Herby crawled to a
sunny rock and sat down. He carefully removed his
muddy boot and tried moving his ankle. " Ouch!" It
hurt too much to move. He pulled off his other boot
and poured the water out of it. After unwrapping the
scarf from his waist, he tossed it aside and peeled off
his wet clothes. He took special care pulling the wet,
clinging pant leg over his injured ankle.

He studied his ankle and wondered if it was
broken. Despite the pain, Herby wiped the scarf and
his clothes in the grass to remove the mud, and then
spread them over some plants. At least the scarf would
dry before the sun disappeared behind the trees.

Still shaking, he looked around for something to
wrap up in. There was nothing. The best he could do
was to stay in the warmth of the sun and shield himself
from the wind. He lay on his side, pressed up against
a stand of dry thick grass. To conserve body heat, he
wrapped his arms around his knees and pulled them to
his chest. *What would I do if some predator came along
right now? Or worse yet, a troop of Girl Scouts?*

After a while, Herby reached over and pulled the
silk scarf to him. It was warm and dry, and he pulled
it over his shivering body. In his mind, he had been
going over some things he learned while working on
his First Aid Merit Badge. *Keep an injured limb elevated
to keep down the swelling.* He lifted his leg and placed it
atop a nearby mushroom. The throbbing pain subsided
somewhat.

Herby didn't feel like moving. With all his heart, he wished that his parents were there to take care of him. But they weren't. There was nobody. He would have to take care of himself.

Shade from the trees slowly crept over him. He noticed that his clothes were also now in the shade. He forced himself up on his hands and knees and crawled over to them. They were still slightly damp, but felt warm, so he decided to put them on. Then he pulled on his right boot, which was also still damp. He didn't even try to put the other boot over his swollen foot and ankle.

With a strip he tore from the scarf, he wrapped his ankle tight enough to keep it from jiggling when he moved, but not so tight that it cut off circulation. He tore off another strip and fashioned it into a backpack for his spare boot and what remained of the scarf.

Herby pulled himself up on one leg. Gritting his teeth against the pain, he hopped over to a bush and studied its lower branches. One that was dead and dry looked like it would make a good crutch. He worked it back and forth until it broke from the bush.

Leaning on his makeshift crutch, Herby slowly began hobbling down the animal trail that followed the river. He stopped only long enough to pick a few seeds to eat and put in his backpack. The abandoned rodent burrows he checked along the trail were either caved in or too small. At last he found one that was suitable. He knew he couldn't be too choosy. The evening chill was beginning to settle, and darkness would soon follow.

...Herby slowly began hobbling down the animal trail...

Herby packed as much dry grass into the hole as he had the strength to gather. The entrance to the burrow was much smaller than the one at Blue Devil Campground. Just three short sticks were needed for a barricade. He also picked a sturdy sharply-pointed stick in case he might need a weapon.

While Herby sat outside the burrow eating his seeds, he pondered his situation. It would take days to walk home, even if he weren't injured. He wouldn't be able to go any distance at all until his ankle was healed. His clothes were scant protection against the cool days of autumn, which come early in the mountains.

Hurting, thirsty, and feeling very dejected, Herby lay down on his stomach and backed into the burrow. There wasn't room enough for him to turn around inside. Anyway, if trouble showed up during the night, he wanted to be facing it. He barricaded the entrance with the sticks and pulled the scarf around himself for warmth. He tried to get comfortable, but the pain in his ankle kept him awake. *Tomorrow, I'll try to find a better place to stay. It will have to be much bigger and closer to water. And there should be plenty to eat nearby. There's no telling how long it'll be before I'm able to travel.*

Herby finally fell into a fitful sleep. Imaginary monsters didn't usually bother him, but tonight one was chasing him in his dreams. As he was trying to run from it, the monster bit him hard on the ankle, and he cried out in pain. With spear in hand, Herby turned to face the ugly, green thing. It growled and clawed at him. He awoke with a start. The monster was real! Something outside was growling and clawing away at the stick barricade.

Chapter 13

Almost Home

"**G**et out of here!" yelled Herby. Surprised at the sound of Herby's voice, the monster stopped for a second. Then it began again and ripped away the barricade. Herby felt its hot, stinking breath as it stuck its snout into the burrow within an inch of his face. He jabbed the sharp stick into the monster's nose. The thing let out a yowl and backed away. By the moonlight, Herby could see that the monster was a bobcat. It hunkered down, glaring back at him.

The cat lunged forward, reaching its paw into the burrow. Herby jabbed hard and felt the stick go deep into the flesh between the cat's toes. With another piercing yowl, the cat backed away. With its ears laid back, it sat bewildered, staring at the burrow and growling. "I told you to get out of here!" yelled Herby. With that, the bobcat bounded away.

Herby cautiously felt around outside for the sticks to his barricade. He could find only one to put back in place. He lay clutching his spear, his heart pounding.

For hours, he listened to the sounds of the night—crickets chirping, an owl hooting in a nearby tree, a coyote howling far away. He heard little things scurrying through the grass. Something big shuffled toward him along the trail. He held his breath and peeked out the burrow's entrance.

Silhouetted in the moonlight, a pokey porcupine shuffled by. When Herby finally drifted off to sleep, birds were singing, and the gray sky was turning pink.

Herby slept soundly all through the morning. A scratching at the burrow's entrance awoke him instantly. He tightened his grip on the stick spear and yelled, "I told you to get out of here! Go away!"

Something whined. "I said go away!" It whined again. *Bobcats don't whine. What's out there?* Again it whined, much louder than before. Herby was afraid to get close enough to the entrance to see what kind of animal it was.

"Whatever you are, go away!" he yelled. This time, there was loud frantic barking.

Herby pulled the stick from the burrow's entrance and poked his head out. "BOZO! Is that you, boy? Is that really you?"

Bozo jumped up and down, wagging his entire body along with his tail. He was in a frenzy of happiness. Herby was both laughing and crying as he dragged himself out of the burrow. Before Herby could pull himself upright, Bozo slurped him with his tongue.

"No, Bozo! Don't do that." Herby used the scarf to wipe the slobbers from his face and hair. Bozo seemed to understand how vulnerable Herby was. Quivering, Bozo could hardly contain himself, but he lay down and waited for Herby to make the next move.

Herby hobbled over to him and hugged his snout. "I never expected to see you out here, Bozo. You just can't know how glad I am to see you." Bozo's tail created a cloud of dust as it thumped wildly against the ground.

"You just can't know how glad I am to see you."

Herby looked Bozo over. "You poor dog. You must have been out here in the wilderness as long as I have." Bozo's thin appearance worried Herby. "And I'll bet you haven't eaten in a long time either." Even if he knew how to hunt, Herby figured a dog as old as Bozo couldn't run fast enough to catch a meal.

Herby thought Bozo must have jumped out of his parents' car at the site of the truck accident. He picked up Herby's scent, but lost it when Herby was swept away in the stream.

Herby guessed, like him, Bozo was on his way home. He had to have traveled all the way around Blue Devil Lake to find him here.

Thinking he might need the crutch again, Herby tied it to Bozo's collar with the scarf. Bozo lay still while Herby climbed up to the back of his neck. Hanging onto Bozo's collar, Herby said, "Okay, pal, let's go home." Bozo stiffly got to his feet. Wagging his tail, he began trotting down the trail.

The hot afternoon sun beat down on the pair. To protect himself from the sun, Herby tied a piece of the scarf around his head, Arabian fashion. Bozo's trotting pained Herby's ankle, but now that Bozo had slowed to a walk, Herby was more comfortable. Occasionally, Bozo turned his head sideways to see if Herby was still there. Herby would pat him and say, "I'm still here, Bozo."

When a side trail branched off toward the river, Bozo followed it. "I'm thirsty, too," said Herby. At the riverbank, the dog obediently laid down at Herby's command. Herby tossed his crutch to the ground and climbed off Bozo's neck.

Bozo politely waited while Herby drank from a little pool at the river's edge. When he had finished, Herby wiped his mouth on his sleeve and said, "It's all yours, boy."

While Bozo was lapping up water, Herby hobbled over to some cattails. He pulled up several young shoots and sloshed them in the water to clean them. He peeled one and called Bozo to him saying, "Try this, Bozo. It's pretty good." Bozo sniffed at the shoot. He looked at Herby quizzically, as if to say, "Do you expect me to *eat* this?"

Bozo turned away and plopped down in the shade of a small willow. While Bozo napped, Herby soaked his ankle in the cold water, knowing it would help bring down the swelling. While soaking, he ate the cattail shoots, including the one that Bozo had refused.

Back on the trail after a good nap, Bozo resumed trotting. Although the rough ride made Herby's ankle hurt more, he didn't try to slow the dog down. By late afternoon, the old dog had once again slowed to a walk.

Suddenly, Bozo stopped and sniffed the air. Herby couldn't smell anything, but thought he heard the faint sound of music. Without warning, Bozo took off in a run. Herby grabbed his collar just in time to keep from falling off.

"Ouch, ouch, ouch," cried Herby as Bozo left the smooth trail to go bounding through the woods. It was nearly dark, and Herby hoped Bozo could see where he was going.

Eventually, Bozo stopped to rest. He stood panting with his tongue hanging out of his mouth. "What got into you, boy?" asked Herby. Bozo sniffed the air again. And Herby heard the music again—only this time, it was louder. He squinted his eyes and looked across the clearing. Something big across the way was all lit up and red and white striped.

Without a word from Herby, Bozo began trotting across the clearing. As they got closer to the bright object, Herby said, "It's a tent, Bozo. It's a big circus tent." Herby remembered seeing the circus posters around Mountainview. They advertised that the circus would be held at the fairgrounds, halfway between Mountainview and the small town of Alpine.

The lights inside the big top made the tent glow in the gathering dark. The parking lot was filled with cars. Herby heard occasional laughter and applause. He wished he were inside too enjoying the performance.

Bozo wove his way between the large circus trucks and trailers. He kept sniffing the air as if he were on to something. Bozo finally stopped at a large cage and stood licking his chops. A tiger in the cage was busily knawing on a large bone. "I know you're hungry, Bozo, but I don't think you want *that* bone," said Herby. The tiger lifted its head and stared at Bozo. It quickly got to its feet and let out a terrible roar. Bozo yelped and ducked under a truck.

When the tiger went back to its bone, Bozo crawled out from under the truck and sniffed the air again. He trotted toward a smaller tent close to the big top. Outside the tent, a fancy French poodle, wearing pink bows on her ears, was eating out of a dish. Bozo ran up and rudely nudged her out of the way. Herby was bounced about and nearly slid off Bozo's neck as the dog began gobbling down the poodle's food. The poodle backed away from Bozo, yapping loudly.

A clown, with orange hair and a big red nose, stepped out of the tent door. "What's the matter, Precious?" he asked. Precious kept yapping. The clown squinted his eyes. "What's that? A strange dog eating your food?" The clown stepped toward Bozo. "Git! Git outta here!" he said. Bozo didn't move. He stood licking his chops and looking up at the clown.

"Hey, mister!" Herby cried out, "Can you help me?"

"Stay right there. Eat all you want," the clown said excitedly. "Don't go away!" The clown disappeared into the tent.

Eat all I want? wondered Herby. Bozo cleaned out the dog dish and moved over to the water bowl while Precious continued yapping.

From inside the tent, Herby heard the clown talking loudly. "Fellas! Come on outside, quick! We got us a new act! There's a real live talking dog out there!"

That clown must not have seen me, thought Herby. *Maybe he needs glasses.*

Seconds later, the clown emerged from the tent, followed by four more clowns. They were all dressed

*Bozo looked up from the water dish to see frightening
creatures descending upon him.*

in funny costumes. One had fuzzy orange hair. Others
had oversized gloves or big floppy shoes. All had big
fake noses and brightly painted faces.

Bozo looked up from the water dish to see
frightening creatures descending upon him. He let
out a yelp and took off running as fast as he could go.
Herby hung onto Bozo's collar for dear life.

Bozo charged through the circus grounds like his
tail was on fire. He knocked over a bucket and sent

it flying. Herby saw an elephant ahead with one foot tied to a stake anchored in the ground. When Bozo ran under its belly, the elephant thrashed its trunk back and forth and trumpeted loudly. That scared Bozo even more.

"Calm down, Bozo," cried Herby.

A man tending the elephant chased Bozo, yelling, "Get out of here, you crazy mutt!"

On and on Bozo ran, until the sounds and smells of the circus were far behind. When it was apparent that he was out of danger, he plopped down in some tall grass, panting heavily.

It was dark, and Herby had no idea where they were. He could see the lighted circus tent behind them in the distance. Town lights glowed in the sky on either side of the tent. But which one was Mountainview? Herby studied the night sky and found the Big Dipper. He hadn't begun work on his Astronomy Merit Badge yet, but he'd read how to find Polaris, the North Star. With

On and on Bozo ran...

his finger, he traced the two stars of the dipper's cup, opposite the handle, straight to Polaris. He looked to the glow in the eastern sky above Mountainview. There was a glow in his heart, too, knowing he was almost home.

After Bozo had rested a while, Herby said, "Come on, boy. We can't stay out in this open meadow. Let's find a good place to spend the night."

Bozo wearily got to his feet. As the old dog ambled along, Herby noticed a flickering light in the woods, and smelled the aroma of a campfire. Bozo must have smelled food. He sniffed the air and trotted toward the camp.

Herby's recent experience had taught him to be wary of strangers. "Slow down, Bozo!" cried Herby. "We don't know what kind of people are there. There could be someone like Jake."

Bozo wasn't listening. He continued trotting toward the camp.

Chapter 14

A Hero's Welcome

A s they got closer, Herby heard familiar voices. Then in the light of the campfire, he saw the purple flag, emblazoned with the outline of an owl's head.

"The Hoot Owls!" cried Herby. "That's my scout patrol, Bozo!"

Just before they entered the light of the campfire, he ordered Bozo to stay. Then, mustering up as much breath as he could hold, Herby gave the patrol call, "Whoooo...Whooo...Whooo."

Nathan stood up and put his hand to his ear. "Hear that owl?"

"Barely," answered Clay. "It must be pretty far away."

Bozo recognized the boys and entered the light, vigorously wagging his tail. Surprised, J.C. stood up and cried, "Bozo! It's Herby's dog, Bozo!"

"Come here, Boy," Jeff said. "Everyone's been looking for you!"

"That poor dog is a mess!" said Tom. "He's covered with cockleburs. And what's he got stuck to his neck?"

"It's me, Herby! It's me stuck to his neck!" All five boys stood frozen in place, with looks of disbelief.

Herby waved his arms above his head. "See? Come closer so you can see it's really me!" The boys gathered around Bozo and squatted down to get a better look.

"I can't believe what I'm seeing," said Clay. "I must be dreaming."

"If you're dreaming, then we all are," remarked Tom.

In a trembling voice, J.C. asked, "How'd you get so small? What on earth did they do to you, Herby?" Tears welled up in his eyes.

"I did it to myself," yelled Herby. "Get me down from here and I'll tell you all about it. And please be careful. My ankle may be broken."

Being the patrol leader, and the oldest, Jeff took charge. He carefully lifted Herby off Bozo and set him on a tree stump a short distance from the fire. Seeing that he was no longer the center of attention, Bozo began sniffing around in the boys' camping gear.

"Do you guys have anything you could feed Bozo?" asked Herby.

"Sure thing," answered Clay as he trotted away from the campfire. "Here's several hot dogs Nathan burned for supper," he hollered. "Do you think Bozo would eat them?"

"Herby says bring them, and bring him something to eat, too," Jeff yelled to Clay. In the meantime, Jeff

took the scout neckerchief from around his neck and
folded it. He laid it on the bill of his cap near Herby.
"Crawl over onto that, Herby. Lean back on the cap
and wrap up in that neckerchief.

"Thanks, Jeff," said Herby as he wrapped up. "This
is real comfy. I was beginning to get a little chilly."

Clay returned with a foil package. "Herby says
he hasn't eaten meat in over a week," said Jeff. "Cut
off the end of one of those hot dogs and carve off the
burned part." Clay did as he was told and handed a tiny
piece to Herby on a toothpick..

"Thanks, Clay," said Herby. "Give the rest of those
to Bozo. You don't need to cut off the burned part for
him. He won't mind." Clay held one out, and Bozo
quickly snapped it up, hardly chewing it before gulping
it down. Wagging his tail, he eagerly awaited the next
hot dog handout.

Clay piled a handful of trail mix on a paper napkin
he placed beside Herby. "You like trail mix, don't you,
Herby?"

Swallowing a mouthful of hot dog, Herby looked
at the pile and answered, "Yeah, but I don't need a
year's supply of it right now."

The boys all laughed. They had gathered around
the stump, sitting on backpacks and rolled-up sleeping
bags. They all started asking questions at once.

"Hold on!" Jeff said. "Let him eat. There'll be
plenty of time for questions when he's finished. Right,
Herby?"

With his mouth full of a piece of dried fruit from
the trail mix, Herby nodded.

"It might be a good idea if we take a look at Herby's ankle while he's eating," said Jeff. "Is that okay, Herby?"

Herby nodded.

"Since you've completed your Medicine Merit Badge, Nathan," Jeff continued, "why don't you do the honors?"

"Be glad to," answered Nathan, who hoped to be a doctor some day. He very carefully pulled the neckerchief away from Herby's ankle. He leaned over Herby and squinted. "I'm going to need a flashlight," Nathan said, "and a magnifying glass."

The response was quick, and Nathan was soon peering down at Herby's ankle. "You've done a great job of wrapping this, Herby." Nathan looked around. "Did anyone happen to bring a pair of tweezers? He's so tiny, I can't undo his bandage without them."

"Here, I'll do it," said Herby, unwrapping the bandage. "I'm finished eating anyway."

After examining the ankle, Nathan announced, "It's purple and very swollen. It needs to be x-rayed. Then we'll know if it's really broken."

"How are they going to do that?" asked Tom. "Herby's so small, an x-ray machine would probably fry him."

"I'll bet my dad could do it," answered J.C. "He says dental x-rays are pretty harmless."

"For now, Herby, keep that ankle wrapped and elevated," said Nathan.

"Does anyone have a cell phone?" asked Herby. "I need to call my parents."

"I do," answered Jeff. "But I tried to make a call before supper and we're out of range. Fisher's Hill is in between Mountainview and us. That must be the problem. One of us can hike up there in the morning and call to have someone pick us up."

"Can't someone go right now?" asked Herby. "They must be awfully worried, and I'd like to get home as soon as possible."

"I'm sorry, Herby," answered Jeff, "but it's just too dangerous to navigate that trail after dark, even with a flashlight. When we were up there this afternoon, we noticed that a big washout had caused several large chunks of trail to slide off into a deep ravine."

"I guess one more night out won't matter that much," said Herby. "What are you guys doing out here, anyway?"

"Looking for you," J.C. answered.

"But look who found who," said Tom.

"They called off the official search for you yesterday," J.C. continued. "The sheriff and half the town have been combing the country ever since you disappeared. He said there was just nowhere else to look."

"Besides, the FBI guys were convinced you had been taken out of the area," Tom added.

"FBI?" asked Herby.

"They were called in because it was a kidnapping," answered Tom. "Lawmen were all over the scene of the truck accident like a bunch of ants. They figured there must have been two kidnappers, and that after one stole the truck he went to their hideout to pick up you and the other kidnapper. They thought that after the accident, one kidnapper took off with you and left the other for dead."

"Is that what happened, Herby?" asked Clay. "That guy they caught who called himself John Smith turned out to be an escaped convict named Archibald Allbad. Of course he denied he ever saw you."

"There was only one kidnapper," said Herby, "and that was Jake."

"Jake?" asked Clay.

"I knew John Smith as Jake Jones, another phony name. And my disappearance didn't start out as a kidnapping. The lady truck driver didn't see me because I was stuffed in Jake's pocket. I'll tell you all about it, but first, what did they do with him?"

"He's in the county jail," answered Jeff. "They're trying to get information out of him before sending him back to prison. There was only one person who claims to have seen you with him. They still have him in the county hospital's psychiatric ward."

"A guy named Bruno?" asked Herby.

"Yeah," answered Jeff. "His name's Bruno."

"I'm not surprised they took him to the hospital after what Jake did to him, but why is he in the psychiatric ward? He seemed perfectly normal to me."

"Well, he didn't seem normal to the doctors," answered Nathan. "He had suffered a bad blow to the head and kept saying your name and swearing that you were only six inches tall."

"Poor Bruno. All he did was try to help me."

"I'm sure he'll be happy that you've been found," said Nathan. "They'll have to believe him now."

While the boys were talking, Bozo squeezed in between J.C. and Tom. He laid his muzzle on the tree stump, wagged his tail, and gazed fondly at Herby. J.C. proceeded to pick off the cockleburs from Bozo's coat and toss them into the campfire.

"Okay, Herby," said Nathan. "Tell us what happened to you. How did you get like this?"

"In a minute. I want to know about my family. Are they all right?"

"They're pretty shaken up," J.C. answered. "Your dad hasn't gone to work since you disappeared. He's been out searching every day. Your mom stays home by the phone. Her eyes are all red from crying. They sent your little sister to stay with your Aunt Bert and Uncle Bud. And, you'll like this. Your grandparents flew in from Arizona. They're staying at your house."

"At least one of us has stopped by your house every day," Clay added. "The whole troop has been out looking for you. The scout picnic was called off as soon as you went missing, and we all searched last weekend and every day after school."

Tom leaned out from the circle and poked the campfire with a stick. "Your folks were really upset about the sheriff calling off the official search."

Jeff nodded. "The troop had a special meeting last night, and everyone voted that we would keep up the search. We mapped out areas that each patrol would be responsible for. Scoutmaster Davidson told your folks the troop would search the whole county again. They were pretty happy to hear that. Every patrol in the troop is out this weekend. Looks like they can all go home early tomorrow."

"Yeah," said Tom. "Hey! Now, we'll have time to see the circus."

"I got to see part of it already," said Herby.

Tom started to ask Herby how he managed to see the circus, but J.C. interrupted. "Your parents were upset about Bozo getting away too."

Bozo's eyes had drooped shut. At the sound of his name, he raised his head to look up at J.C.

"They took Bozo with them to the accident scene," continued J.C., "and as soon as they got there, he jumped out the window and was off like a shot. Your dad said when Bozo got your scent, he went nuts. He charged through a culvert under the highway and got caught in a stream. They said the last time they saw him, Bozo had climbed out of the stream and ran off. They called and called for him, but he wouldn't come back. He just kept sniffing and running until he disappeared into the woods."

"It's a good thing for me that Bozo *didn't* go back. After I hurt my ankle, I wasn't sure I'd ever make it home. Bozo probably saved my life. And I'll tell you something else. If it hadn't been for the stuff I've learned in scouting, I wouldn't have lasted out there any time at all."

"Hear that, guys?" said Jeff. "We never know when our scouting skills will be put to the test."

"Getting back to Bozo," said Clay, "your parents were really sad that they lost him. They know how much he means to you. They were on television every night and—"

"My parents were on television?" interrupted Herby.

"Yes," answered Clay. "Every night. They showed your picture and asked people to help look for you. Your parents showed Bozo's picture, too, and asked people to look for him."

"They showed my picture?" asked Herby. "I hope it was a good one."

"Not really," answered Tom. "It looked too much like you." After the laughter died down, Tom continued. "They made a big to-do about you at school, too. Mr. Smothers called a special assembly. You should have seen the girls blubbering all over the place."

"They were crying?" asked Herby. "About me?"

"Yeah," answered Tom, moving his eyebrows up and down, "especially Debbie."

"*Really?*" A huge smile lit up Herby's face. Somebody snickered, and Herby was embarrassed that he had appeared overly interested.

"Come on, Herby!" pleaded Nathan. "Tell us what happened to you!"

Herby began. The boys all gathered in close to hear, hanging on his every word. Apparently feeling suffocated by the closeness, Bozo squeezed out of

The boys all gathered in close to hear...

the ring. After curling up on an open sleeping bag, he began snoring noisily.

Herby awoke the next morning to the clatter of metal utensils. The boys were up and fixing breakfast. It had been nearly midnight before they had all settled down to sleep, and Herby had talked until he was hoarse.

Herby crawled out from under Jeff's cap, which had served as a tent. "Mornin', Herby," said Clay. "How'd you sleep?"

"That's the best sleep I've had in more than a week," Herby yelled. "It's the first night I've felt safe. Jeff's neckerchief made a really good sleeping bag, too."

Bozo had spent the night curled up next to the tree stump and jumped to his feet at the sound of Herby's voice. With his tail wagging, he put his muzzle on the stump. Herby patted him and said, "Good old Bozo. You're the best dog ever."

Clay brought Herby a small cup filled with water, a pinch of soap, and a scrap of paper towel. "Breakfast is almost ready, Herby," he said. "Better get washed up."

"How about some oatmeal?" J.C. asked as he set a tiny bowl, fashioned out of foil, down on the stump next to Herby. "I stuck that piece of toothpick in there for you to use as a spoon. We've got hot chocolate, too, but how would you drink it?"

"I've been drinking out of a plastic soda bottle cap," answered Herby. "Do you have one?"

"Great idea!" J.C. soon returned with a capful of piping hot chocolate.

All the boys except Jeff gathered around the stump to join Herby for breakfast. "Nathan cooked some more hot dogs for Bozo's breakfast," said Clay.

"Yeah, just the way he likes them—burned," Tom remarked.

"Thanks, Nathan," said Herby. "Where's Jeff?"

"He was gone before any of us got up," answered Tom. "He must have hiked up to the top of Fisher's Hill so he could use his cell phone."

The boys had not quite finished their breakfast when Bozo jumped to his feet and started barking. Jeff strode into camp. "Don't worry, Bozo. It's just me. Hey, did you guys leave me anything to eat?" Jeff picked up the pan of oatmeal from where it sat on a warm stone near the fire. He carried it to the tree stump and ate right out of the pan.

"Did your phone work?" asked Herby. "Will someone be picking us up soon?"

"Sure thing," answered Jeff. "I talked to your dad."

"Did you tell him about how Herby was all shrunk up?" asked Clay.

"No way!" answered Jeff. "I didn't want to be responsible for giving Herby's dad a heart attack. I just told him that Bozo had found Herby and that they were both okay."

"I guess this *is* going to be a shock for them," said Herby.

"You think?" asked Tom.

Chapter 15

Home at Last

The boys had their gear all packed and ready to go by the time the big four-wheel vehicle rumbled into camp with Tom's dad at the wheel. Herby's dad jumped out before it had completely rolled to a stop. He looked back and forth at the boys. "Well, where is he? Where's Herby?"

A tiny voice called from the stump, "I'm here, Dad."

Herby's dad looked in the direction of the stump, but over it and into the woods. "What are you doing in the woods?" he yelled. "Come here and give me a big hug!"

"I'm afraid he can't do that, sir," Jeff said with a serious tone in his voice.

The smile fell from Herby's dad's face. "Why not? What's wrong with him?"

Herby climbed onto Bozo's neck. "Go to Dad," he ordered. Bozo trotted over to Herby's father, who hardly noticed him. He was still looking out into the woods.

"Dad! Look down here! Here I am on Bozo!"

Herby saw a look of horror come over his dad's face as he dropped to his knees. "MY GOD!" he cried. "What have those monsters done to you?"

On the drive back to town, Herby sat nestled in his dad's shirt collar and talked into his left ear. As Herby told him the whole story, his dad had little to say. Herby couldn't help but notice the tear that escaped from his dad's left eye and ran down his cheek.

Herby's dad was still in a state of shock when the truck rolled into Mountainview. "Could you please drop Herby and me off last?" he asked. "I've got to have time to think of some way to break this to my wife." Herby, too, had been wondering how his mom was going to react.

As the boys were dropped off at their homes, each one came to the window to say goodbye to Herby and tell him how glad they were to have him back. Finally, only Tom and Bozo remained in the back. They were about a block from Herby's home when his dad said to Tom's father, "Maybe we'd better get out here. Herby's mom and grandparents will probably be on the front porch waiting for us. If they see me get out, and don't see Herby, it might frighten them. They may think the worst. I'm going to slip in the back door and then call them into the house."

They got out of the vehicle, and from his dad's coat pocket, Herby watched as Tom opened the back door for Bozo to hop out. Tom slammed the door shut and leaned out of the window. "While we were all riding back here, we pretty much got the rest of the cockleburs off Bozo. But he could sure use a bath. If it's all right with you, Mr. Strange, I can come over to your place this afternoon and give him one."

Herby said, "I thought you wanted to see the circus."

"I can see a circus any old day," answered Tom. "But how often does a guy get to soap up a celebrity? You know, Herby, you and Bozo are both going to be famous once everybody gets wind of all this."

"I'm afraid you're right, Tom," said Herby's dad. "If you want to give Bozo a bath, that's great. He and the rest of the family would appreciate it very much."

"Thanks a lot, Tom," said Herby. "Bathing Bozo is my job, so I really appreciate it. See ya later then."

Herby's dad walked down the back alley with Herby riding in his coat pocket. There was a strange van parked in the alley behind the house. Too late, Dad saw that it was a news van. A woman with a microphone jumped out of the front door, and a man with a news camera jumped out of another.

"Quick, Herby," said Dad. "Get down, so they can't see you."

The woman walked up to Herby's dad and stuck the mike in his face. "Good morning, Mr. Strange. I'm Shelly Myers, BNS National News Service. Is there any news to report on your son's kidnapping? Have the kidnappers made contact yet?"

Herby could hear the whir of the camera running.

"Well, I do have some news. This is Herby's dog, Bozo. Herby's Boy Scout Patrol found him a few miles outside of town last night." The cameraman quickly turned toward Bozo. Bozo didn't like the black, whirring, one-eyed thing in his face. He growled and bared his teeth. The cameraman quickly stepped back and then turned his focus on Herby's dad.

"I'm sure you're happy to have your son's dog back," said the lady reporter. "Is there anything else you can tell us at this time?"

"No. I haven't anymore to say right now. Good day," said Herby's dad as he stepped into the backyard and closed the gate.

"You handled that pretty well, Dad," said Herby as they neared the house.

"We can't hold them off forever. The news people have been very helpful in the search for you. But we have enough to deal with right now."

Herby's dad quietly entered through the back door. There seemed to be no one in the house. He peeked out the front window. "Your Aunt Bert and Suzanne are out there, too, Herby. Your mom must have called them with the news and—Oh no! The Duffy's from next door are out there, too. I'm going to have to think of a way to get them to leave. This particular family reunion needs some privacy."

"Dad? May I get out of your pocket now? My ankle hurts from all the jostling."

"Oh, I'm sorry. Let's make you comfortable before we get everyone in here."

Herby's dad arranged a dinner napkin inside a salad bowl. He placed the bowl near the flower bouquet on the dining room table. Then he gently lifted Herby out of his pocket and set him on the napkin. He propped up the napkin behind Herby's back and laid a corner of it over the rim of the bowl where Herby could rest his ankle. "We're going to have the doc take a look at that ankle right away."

Herby could hear his dad from the kitchen, talking on the wall phone. "Hello, Dr. Bloomquist? This is John Strange. You told me to call you any time of the day or night to check out Herby whenever we got him back. Yes...yes, just this morning. He may have a broken ankle. Well, yes, there is something else wrong with him, but I think he'll have to see a specialist for it. No. I don't want to describe his symptoms over the phone. It's too hard to believe—I mean too hard to describe. Great! We'll see you within an hour then. Oh, by the way, the press is camped outside. They don't know yet that we have Herby. We need some private time before we tell everyone, okay? Thanks, Doctor. We'll see you soon."

Dad came back into the dining room. "Are you ready for me to get the family now, Herby? I'm sure you realize this isn't going to be easy."

"I'm ready, Dad. I know it'll be a shock for them to see me like this, but I'll sure be glad to see them all."

Herby heard the front door open and his dad say, "Won't you all please come in?"

"How did you get in the house without our seeing you?" asked Grandpa.

"Where's Herby?" cried his mom.

"Patience, patience," said Dad. "He's waiting in the dining room. But please don't anyone go in there just yet. Thank you for stopping by, Mr. and Mrs. Duffy. We'll see you later."

Refusing to wait another minute to see her son, Herby's mom rushed into the dining room. She wildly scanned the room, and then her eyes fell upon Herby. There he was, sitting in a bowl in the middle of the dining room table next to a bouquet of flowers. She did what any mother would do under the circumstances. She screamed hysterically. Predictably, the rest of the family rushed into the room to see what the screaming was about. Aunt Bert and Suzanne joined in the hysterical chorus. Herby's grandpa was the only one who seemed to have lost his voice.

"Oh, no!" said Dad as he rushed into the dining room. Evidently in his rush, Dad had not closed the front door, because Mr. and Mrs. Duffy were right behind him.

Dad managed to get everyone quieted down. He stood behind the chair of his sobbing wife and put his hands on her shoulders. "Now, now, everyone, let's please have no more hysterics," he said. "Herby's ankle may just be sprained."

"*His ankle!*" exclaimed Grandpa. "It appears the boy has a problem a bit more serious than that!"

"Well, yes, he does," said Dad. "But let's just all be calm and take one thing at a time. Now, Herby's going to start at the beginning and tell us the whole story. You'll all have to be very quiet. His voice is also very small."

"Dad? May I do something before I begin?"

"What is it, Herby?"

"I want to hug Mom."

Herby crawled over to his mother and wrapped his arms around her hand. She laid her head on the table and wept as Herby kissed her cheek. "I'm so sorry, Mom," said Herby through his own tears. "I'm so sorry to have caused everyone so much trouble."

"My dear, sweet boy." She gently kissed him on his head. "Sit on my hand, sweetie, and let me put you back in the bowl so we can hear what you have to say."

Everyone in the room was spellbound as Herby told his story. For once, his little sister, Suzanne, listened quietly and didn't interrupt. Herby was just finishing his story when the doorbell rang. His Dad quickly turned to answer it and bumped into the Duffys, still standing behind him.

"Excuse me. Have you been here the whole time?"

"Yes," said Mrs. Duffy, wiping the tears from her eyes. She grabbed Mr. Duffy by the arm and headed for the door. "We'll be on our way now. We don't wish to intrude."

Herby heard Mrs. Duffy say from the front room, "Why, hello, Dr. Bloomquist. You've got your work cut out for you on this one. I certainly hope you know what you're doing."

Everyone in the room was spellbound as Herby told his story.

Carrying his black bag, Dr. Bloomquist had a puzzled look on his face when he came into the dining room followed by Herby's dad. "What on earth did she mean by that, John?" he asked.

After one look at Herby, Dr. Bloomquist had to sit down and take his own pulse. When he regained his composure, he said, "I'll need a magnifying glass to examine his ankle."

Suzanne ran to the desk in the next room and brought one back.

"Thank you, Suzanne." Using the glass, the doctor looked at Herby's ankle. "Whoever wrapped this bandage did an excellent job."

"Thank you," said Herby. "I learned that while working on my scout First Aid Merit Badge."

"Verrry good. I think I have some tweezers here in my bag. I'll need to remove that bandage."

"Don't bother, Doctor, I can do it," said Herby as he unwrapped his ankle.

"Hmmm," said the doctor. "I doubt if it's broken since you're able to move it somewhat. I would ordinarily have it x-rayed, but under the circumstances, that would be impossible."

"Would an x-ray machine like they use in a dental office be okay?" asked Herby.

"What a splendid idea! Dental x-rays are mild and virtually harmless. I'll make the arrangements with your dentist and plan to be there myself. In the meantime, keep that ankle wrapped and elevated." Dr. Bloomquist snapped his black bag shut and then gave Herby a very serious look. "Now, young man, do you want to tell me what in the world those kidnappers did to you?"

Herby was beginning to feel like a stuck disc as he once again told his story.

As Dad escorted Dr. Bloomquist to the door, the doctor spoke in a hushed voice, but Herby heard him anyway. "I'm afraid a treatment for Herby's more obvious ailment is beyond anything known to medical science. I suggest that a team of research scientists be assembled to develop an antidote to Herby's formula. I'll do some research myself to see if I can come up with some names for you."

As the two men got nearer the front door, Herby strained to hear the rest of the conversation. Suddenly his father cried out, "Oh, no!"

Chapter 16

Quite a Day

When the front door opened, Herby could hear yelling and loud talking outside. He heard Dr. Bloomquist say, "Go back inside to your family, John. I'll take care of it."

"Thanks, Doctor, I can't handle all of this right now."

Suzanne let out a piercing scream. "Mommy, Mommy," she cried. "A strange man is looking in the window!"

Dad stomped back into the dining room. "That does it!" He pulled the blinds down, jerked the drapes shut, and then marched into the next room to do the same.

"John, what's going on?" Mom called.

"It's those darned nosey neighbors!" he yelled as he strode back into the room. "It was bad enough all week with people slowly driving by and gawking at the house."

"Calm down, Son," said Grandpa.

"Calm down, you say. Those two busy bodies have drawn a crowd out there in the yard! Cars are lining up on both sides of the street! The Duffys are out there in front of the TV cameras, blabbing to those reporters."

Mom got up to answer the phone, which had been ringing all the while Dad had been talking. She had no sooner hung up from that call, than it rang again. "Who *are* these people?" she said after the second call.

The phone rang again. Dad grabbed it up and said gruffly, "Now, listen here—Bud? Oh, it's you. I'm glad you finally got our message. Yes, your nephew's back home. Of course, come right over. Bert's already here. Herby is eager to see you, too. There's quite a hubbub outside the house right now, so you'll have to park several blocks away and slip in the back way."

Later, after Dad had let Uncle Bud in the back door, he kept him in the kitchen for quite a while. Even after Dad explained to him all that had happened, Bud was still shocked when he entered the dining room.

After Herby and Bud exchanged greetings, Dad asked, "Did you have any trouble getting to the house, Bud?"

"No. As a matter of fact, I was able to slip through a TV crew and a number of reporters without being noticed. They were all busy interviewing some kid in your backyard who was giving Bozo a bath."

"Hey," yelled Herby. "Maybe they'll have Bozo and Tom on the six o'clock news."

Bud pulled a chair up to the table. "You've had quite an adventure, Herby. Tell me about this boat you built. And did you really sail it clear across Blue Devil Lake?"

"Yep. I tried to remember all the stuff you taught me about sailing. If it hadn't been for you, Uncle Bud, I'd still be out there trying to walk all the way around the lake." When Herby got to the part in his story about going over the spillway, he hesitated. "Say, Uncle Bud, you spend a lot of time up at the lake. Do you know anything about the guy who owns the boat repair shop? A guy named Grady O'Sullivan?"

"Grady? Sure I know him. He's a good friend of mine. But how do *you* know him? Did you stop by to have your little boat repaired?"

Herby laughed. "No, I don't know him, but I think I know someone who does. Tell me about Grady."

"I met him about three years ago. He had come to the U.S. several years before from Ireland. He said he'd traveled quite a bit and liked these parts better than anyplace else he'd been. So that's why he settled up at the lake. He worked for the former owner of the boat repair shop up there, and bought him out when he retired last year. Grady married the old man's daughter, a real cute little gal, a couple of years ago. They have a little boy, about six months old now. So, Herby, who is it you think knows him?"

"Remember the old man from Ireland who thought I was a leprechaun? Well, I think Grady is the son the old man has spent years looking for."

"No kidding," said Uncle Bud. "How can we get hold of this old man?"

"He doesn't have a telephone," answered Herby. "And I don't think I can find the apartment building where he lives. I met him in some little park in the older part of town."

Bozo whined at the back door, and Dad left the table for a minute to let him in the house. Bozo's coat was now clean and fluffy, and he went from one family member to another to be patted and have praises whispered to him.

"Was it Founder's Park?" asked Grandpa.

"Maybe," answered Herby. "It was just a few blocks from the recycling plant."

"That's it," said Grandpa. "In my younger years, I had a job near the park. I used to eat my lunch there every day. I remember one time I—"

Herby's grandma interrupted. "Later, dear. Right now, we need to talk about how to reunite the O'Sullivans."

"Oh, excuse me," said Grandpa.

"Anyway, the old man says he goes to the park every day to feed the pigeons," Herby continued. "I bet if Grady went to the park and watched for him, they'd meet up. Would you call Grady, Uncle Bud?"

"You bet. I'll do it right now. If Grady is his son, you've made some people very happy."

"You better keep that mean old man away from Herby," Suzanne piped up. "He might try to put him back in that rusty old birdcage."

Bud returned to the dining room. "Grady was so happy with the news he could hardly contain himself. When a friend of his visited Ireland a couple of years ago, he tried to look up Grady's father for him, but no one in his little village knew where he was. He had just disappeared. Grady's going to the park right now to look for him. I said your Aunt Bert and I would meet him there to help search."

"That's *great*, Uncle Bud!" said Herby. "Can I go too? I know what he looks like."

"You'd better stay here, Herby. You just got home, remember? And I think you've probably had enough excitement for a while. Grady's bringing some photographs of the old man. Don't worry, we'll find him."

"I hope I get to see him again. I need to apologize to him. And I want to thank him for the clothes and boots he made for me."

"When we find him, I'll tell him that for you. Those clothes and boots look like they've been through a war."

"Yeah, they're pretty much worn out," said Herby. "I'm going to miss the boots. I wish I had another pair just like them."

"Well, we'd better get going," Bud said to Bert.

Aunt Bert leaned over and lightly patted Herby on the head with her forefinger. "Now, you get some rest. We'll check in on you tomorrow."

"Let's see if we can sneak out the back door," said Uncle Bud.

Ordinarily, Herby would have been bored with nothing to do but sit, but there was plenty to occupy his mind. Throughout the afternoon, one of his parents was on the telephone, either answering or making calls. And every few minutes the doorbell rang. Grandpa would peer out from the curtains to see who it was. Then he'd go to the door and yell, "Go away and leave us alone!" Sometimes, it was a friend or neighbor bringing food. Then Grandpa would take the dish and politely thank them.

From the backyard, Bozo did a pretty good job keeping intruders away. *I wonder if dogs lose their voices when they bark too much,* thought Herby.

For quite a while, Herby could hear Suzanne whining and crying. She seemed to be pleading first with Mom and then with Dad. The house quieted down somewhat after she was finally sent to her room.

Grandma stopped by to check on Herby. "What was wrong with Suzanne?" he asked. "I couldn't quite hear."

"She was upset because your parents wouldn't let her take you around the neighborhood to show you to all her friends."

Finally it was dinnertime and the family was again seated around the table. "It's a good thing people are still bringing food," said Mom. "With all that's going on, I don't know when I could have found time to cook."

"I don't know how we can even get out of the house to go to the store," said Dad. "We seem to be prisoners in our own home."

Just as Dad was about to take a bite of food, the telephone rang again. He slammed his fork down. "That does it!" He left the room and returned a few minutes later. "I've unplugged all the phones in the house. Only our closest friends and neighbors know our cell phone number. Perhaps now we can eat in peace."

"Where is Herby going to sleep tonight?" asked Grandma.

"I know where he can sleep," Suzanne piped up. "In my dollhouse!"

"No way!" said Herby. "Why can't I sleep in my own room?"

"With all those critters you have in there?" asked Grandma. "That snake of yours might make a meal of you."

"Suzanne has a good idea, Herby," said Mom. "You could be very comfortable in her dollhouse. Everything is just about your size. Will you at least try it?"

"I guess so. But can we put the dollhouse down here in the den?"

"Considering your condition, I don't think you should be in a room by yourself, Herby."

"Bozo can stay with him," suggested Grandpa. "He's done a pretty good job of watching out for Herby so far."

Everyone agreed with Grandpa's suggestion. After dinner, Dad went upstairs and returned with the dollhouse. He placed it on the coffee table and lifted Herby inside. Herby hopped over to a tiny chair and sat down. "I guess this won't be too bad." Across the room of the dollhouse sat Suzanne's doll, grinning back at Herby. "But *she's* going to have to go."

"She's *not* going to go!" cried Suzanne. "This is Marci's house, and you are her guest!"

"This might be a good time for Marci to take a trip," Mom said. "Herby could house-sit for her while she's gone."

Suzanne thought for a moment. "Marci could go to Paris!" Suzanne reached into the dollhouse for Marci and then scampered away. "If Marci's going to take a trip to Paris, I've got to get her prettiest clothes packed."

Grandma poked at the doll's bed with her finger. "This bed will never do."

Mom lifted the doll's plastic bathtub from its place and held it up to the light. "This looks like it will hold water all right," she said as she left the room with the little tub. She returned with it filled with warm water, a washcloth to serve as a towel, a tiny piece of soap, and a large dishtowel. As she set the bathtub in its place, she said to Herby, "You could use a nice, warm bath. Take off those dirty rags and toss them out here.

"Right here in front of everyone?"

"That's what this dishtowel is for," answered Mom, as she draped the towel over the open side of the dollhouse. "There. Now you can have some privacy. Can you see all right?"

"Thanks, Mom. The light shines through just fine."

Herby peeled off his ragged clothes and tossed them out from behind the towel. "What am I supposed to wear now?"

"I think Suzanne's doll clothes might fit you," answered Mom.

"Marci's clothes?" wailed Herby. "I can't wear *girl's* clothes!"

"I'm sure we can find something suitable," said Mom. "We'll see."

While Herby was bathing, his dad cut a tiny mattress from a new sponge he had bought for washing the car. Grandpa donated a couple of clean handkerchiefs for sheets. The doll's bed already had a blanket.

After bathing and drying off, Herby called out, "I'm all finished. What now?"

His mom handed him a piece of clothing under the dishtowel. He held it up to inspect it.

It was a frilly, flannel nightgown. Before he could say anything, Mom said, "Notice how nice and warm the nightgown is? After I washed it, I dried it with the hair dryer."

I guess I can't be too choosy, thought Herby as he put on the nightgown.

"I'm dressed, " he called out. "You can take the dishtowel away now."

"Go into the next room and see what a nice bed we've made for you, Herby," said Grandma. "The blanket is warm, too, after being washed and dried. And there's a surprise for you on the night stand."

Herby hopped into the dollhouse bedroom and sat down on the bed. He bounced up and down a couple of times. "This feels great! Especially after the way I've had to sleep these past few nights." On the nightstand next to the bed, sat a tiny teacup filled with steaming, hot milk. Next to it was a matching plate of cookie crumbs.

Mom handed Herby a piece of elastic bandage. "You'd better wrap your ankle up right away."

As Herby did so, he said, "Thanks, everyone. It sure feels good to be home."

While Herby ate, Suzanne came bouncing back into the den. Seeing the dishes he was using, she exclaimed. "Those are dishes from Marci's kitchen!"

"We didn't think Marci would mind," said Grandma.

"Noooo, I don't think she'd mind," said Suzanne. "But Marci *did* mind that Mommy took some of her clothes for Herby. But Mommy said she would get her some new ones. That made Marci happy." Suzanne stuck her face in the dollhouse. "And I'm happy you're home, Herby, even if you are all shrunk up. I've missed you."

"I've missed you too, squirt. Thanks for letting me use your dollhouse and stuff. It's really nice and comfortable in here."

After the warm bath and warm milk, Herby felt very tired. He yawned a big yawn.

"I think it's time we all turned in for the night," said Dad. "This has been quite a day!"

"I've missed you too, squirt."

Suzanne, Grandma, and Grandpa told Herby
goodnight and went upstairs. His mom tucked him into
bed and gently patted him."

"Gee, Mom," said Herby. "You haven't tucked me
in since I was a little kid."

"I know," she said, wiping her eyes. "Goodnight,
my little man."

165

As soon as Mom stepped away, Bozo stuck his head in the dollhouse and wagged his tail.

Herby reached out and patted his nose. "How's my old pal?"

"I'm leaving the light on in here," Dad said. "If you need anything at all, send Bozo upstairs."

"I will, Dad," Herby sleepily mumbled.

"Sleep well, my son," said Dad. "I thank God that you're home safe."

Dad reached down with both hands and scratched Bozo behind his ears. "And thank you, Bozo. You'll watch after him for us won't you, boy?"

"Woof," answered Bozo.

Chapter 17

Herby Meets the Mayor

Herby was awakened early in the morning by the ringing of the doorbell. Bozo jumped up from his place near the dollhouse and ran to the door barking. Soon Dad came bounding down the stairs, tying the belt to his bathrobe. Entering the room, he looked at Herby sitting on the edge of his bed. "Are you all right?"

"Yup. There's someone at the front door."

"It must be one of those pesky reporters." Dad stomped off toward the door mumbling. "How rude of them to bother us this early in the morning!"

Herby stuck his head out of the dollhouse to see who it was.

"Quiet, Bozo!" said Dad. "Why, *Mayor Farnsworth!* What brings you out this time of day?"

"I know it's early. I apologize and hope I didn't wake you. But I have some very important things to discuss with you. I tried to call, but apparently your phone has been disconnected."

"I unplugged all the phones. It was the only way we could get any peace. I'm sorry if it inconvenienced you, Mayor."

"That's quite all right. I certainly understand. Ever since the six o'clock news yesterday evening, my phone hasn't stopped ringing. May I come in?"

"Excuse my bad manners. Of course you may."

As soon as the mayor stepped inside, Bozo busily began sniffing his shoes and pants.

"How's your son after his ordeal?" asked the mayor.

"Except for what might be a broken ankle, he seems to be fine. Our doctor checked him over as best he could."

"That's good to hear. Is Herby up yet?"

"Why, yes, he's awake. Why do you ask?"

"Since what I have to say concerns him, I think he should be present."

"Of course, Mayor, he's in the den. Come right this way."

Herby pulled his head back into the dollhouse. *The mayor of Mountainview wants to talk to me? Oh, no! And here I am in this sissy nightgown.*

Quickly hopping back to his bed, Herby jerked the blanket off and wrapped it around himself to hide the nightgown. He hopped over to a dollhouse chair and sat down. He had just enough time to spit in his hand and slick down his hair before the two men appeared.

Bozo continued sniffing as the mayor looked around the room. "You say Herby is in here?" asked the mayor.

Dad pointed to the open dollhouse, where Herby sat waiting. The mayor's mouth dropped open and his eyes nearly popped out of his head. "Oh, my goodness!" he cried.

Dad pulled a chair up to the dollhouse. "Here, Mayor Farnsworth, I think you need to sit down."

After seating himself, the mayor took a handkerchief from his pocket and wiped his brow. "The old couple on the news said your boy had shrunk," he said, "but I assumed they were exaggerating."

Just then, Herby's mom entered the den carrying a tray. The mayor stood up and said, "You must be Mrs. Strange."

"Yes, this is my wife, Lisa," said Dad. "Lisa, may I present Mayor Farnsworth?"

"I'm honored to meet you, Mayor. " She set the tray down on a nearby table. Would you care for a cup of coffee and some homemade oatmeal cookies?"

"Why, yes, I certainly would."

After serving the men, Mom set a tiny cup of milk and a plate of cookie crumbs on the dollhouse table next to Herby. "Good morning, Herby," she whispered. "How are you this morning?"

"I'm fine, Mom, but I sure could use some clothes."

"I have some for you," she whispered. "I'll be right back with them and the dishtowel so you can get dressed."

"Thanks, Mom, and thanks for the milk and cookies."

The mayor must have been hungry. He ate four big cookies, one after another. He dropped the fifth cookie, which was quickly snapped up by Bozo. In the meantime, Mom laid some doll clothes on Herby's bed. As she draped the dishtowel over the dollhouse, she turned to the mayor and said, "Please excuse Herby for a few minutes. He was uncomfortable about not being dressed."

"That's quite all right. I'll just have another one of your delicious cookies."

Herby quickly put on a pair of pants and a T-shirt. He looked in the mirror on the dollhouse wall. *Say, these fit pretty well. That doll is taller than I am, but these pants are just the right length.* There was even a pair of socks and slip-on shoes. The shoes were rather large, but the left one fit over his swollen foot just fine. *I wish the boots the old man made for me weren't all worn out.* When he had finished dressing, he called out, "I'm ready."

As Mom removed the dishtowel, Dad said, "I'm sorry, Mayor, that I haven't formally introduced my son. This, of course, is Herby. Herby, this is Mayor Farnsworth."

Herby hopped forward and stretched out his open hand. "Glad to meet you, Mr. Mayor." Herby had been taught that it was good manners to shake hands when being introduced. But he now felt very stupid for offering his hand.

Smiling, the mayor leaned forward in his chair and held out his little finger. Herby used both hands to pump the finger up and down. "I'm glad to meet

"Glad to meet you, Mr. Mayor."

you, too, Herby. I guess you know that you're a very
famous person."

"I *am?*"

"Of course. I can't imagine how you did it, but
no one else in history has ever actually shrunk a living
being."

171

Dad pulled a chair over to the dollhouse for Mom. "What important things did you want to discuss with us, Mayor?" he asked.

"Well, since all the major networks and radio stations have been unable to contact you, they've all been calling me. It began after the six o'clock news yesterday evening. The calls haven't let up since."

"I'm so sorry you've been bothered by all this," said Mom.

"Don't give it a second thought, my dear! It's the kind of bother this town could use more of. Why, Herby has put this town on the map! All these media people are headed for Mountainview. They all want the opportunity to interview Herby. Most would like to interview him in his laboratory, where he actually developed his formula."

"When did they want to do all this?" asked Dad.

"Why, today! That's why I'm here. I thought you should have some advance notice."

"*Today!*" exclaimed Mom. "I should say not! Herby hasn't even been home twenty-four hours! After all he's been through he needs time to recuperate. We all need time to recuperate."

"But, Mrs. Strange," stammered the mayor, "you know how media people are. They want the news *now* while it's still news! These people are on their way to Mountainview as we speak."

"Lisa, if Herby feels up to it, I think we'd better let him do it," said Dad. "You know the media will be hounding us until it's done. The sooner we get it

over with, the sooner our lives can return to normal."
Lowering his voice, he said, "That is, if they can *ever*
return to normal."

During the conversation, Herby's grandparents
had entered the room and seated themselves near the
dollhouse.

"Has anyone thought to ask Herby?" said Grandpa.
"Shouldn't he have something to say on the matter?"

"You don't have to worry about me, Mom," said
Herby. "I feel fine. But it *is* kind of scary to think about
being on TV."

"You'll do just fine," said the mayor, "just fine.
They'll ask the questions, and all you have to do is
answer them."

"And think of all the publicity Herby will have,"
added Grandpa. "I'll bet he won't have to win any
science fairs to get offered full scholarships to the very
best schools in the nation."

"Yeah," said Herby excitedly. "May I do it, Mom?
May I?"

"We haven't discussed this yet, but it's something
we can't ignore," said Mom. "In your small state, Herby,
you are extremely vulnerable. Unless and until you can
be returned to normal size, I don't see how you can
even *go* to school. And I certainly don't want you in
a room full of rowdy reporters. One accidental bump
with a microphone or an elbow could kill you."

"I know how we can make it safe, Mom. I can get
in one of my animal cages during the interviews. In
fact, I've got an empty one right now."

"That's a good idea," said Dad. "I'll get the cage cleaned."

"The TV technicians will probably need to set up their equipment in advance of the interviews," commented the mayor. "Is there an entrance they can use that won't disturb the family?"

"Yes," answered Dad. "I'm glad you asked. There's an outside stairway at the back of the house going up to Herby's room. They can use that, and they won't need to enter the rest of the house at all."

"Well, I'm glad for that!" said Mom. "There is one condition," she added. "For Herby's safety, his father will be on one side of him during the interviews, and I will be on the other."

"A very sound idea," said the mayor. "In fact, to insure his safety, I volunteer to stand behind Herby between the two of you." With that, the mayor got up to leave.

"Would you care to join us for breakfast, Mayor?" asked Grandma. "I'm going to fix my famous banana nut pancakes. They're Herby's favorite."

"Why, thank you, Ma' am, how kind of you. But I need to take a suit to the cleaners right away and then get to the barbershop. As the representative of our great town, I want to make a good impression on national TV!"

Chapter 18

A Reunion

With a grandiose wave of his hand, the mayor was out the door.

"What a thoughtful man, to be so concerned with Herby's safety," commented Grandma.

"Part of that concern may be due to the mayor's plans to run for state representative next year," said Dad. "I'm sure he won't mind all the publicity and TV exposure."

Dad plugged the phones back in and then had to excuse himself from the breakfast table to answer a call. In a few minutes, he returned to announce, "That was Dr. Bloomquist. He'll meet Herby and me at Dr. Sutton's office at 8:30 this morning to have Herby's ankle x-rayed."

When Herby and his dad later arrived at the dentist's office, Dr. Bloomquist met them at the door. "Follow me. Dr. Sutton has everything ready for us."

Dr. Sutton was adjusting the x-ray machine as they entered the room with Herby looking out from Dad's shirt pocket. "Good morning, John," he said.

Dr. Sutton peered behind Dad and Dr. Bloomquist, looking for Herby. "Good morning, Dr. Sutton," yelled Herby. With his mouth gaping open, the Doctor stared at Dad's pocket for a second before he was able to speak. "And—and good morning to you, Herby. I can't tell you how good it is to see you back home again."

"Thank you, sir. It sure is good to be back."

"J.C. was so excited when he got home yesterday," Dr. Sutton continued. "He told me all about your adventures. But I must admit, it's unnerving to see how small you've become."

Dr. Sutton placed a towel on the instrument tray beneath the x-ray machine. "Here, John, set Herby down on this."

"I have great news for you two," said Dr. Bloomquist as he maneuvered Herby's leg into position. "I was able to get in touch with Dr. Vanderpool, one of the nation's leading medical researchers. He saw your story on the news last night and is extremely interested in Herby's case. In fact he's been trying to get in touch with you. He wants to know if Herby can come to San Diego right away."

The doctor repositioned Herby's leg so that Dr. Sutton could take more x-rays.

"Go to San Diego?" asked Dad. "Does he really think he can help Herby?"

"Yes. He and his team are almost certain they can."

"That's wonderful news," said Dad. "Did he happen to mention what his fee might be? Our medical insurance probably doesn't cover Herby's particular disability."

"Don't give cost a second thought. Dr. Vanderpool said he considers this a great opportunity to advance scientific knowledge. It turns out his team has also developed a formula to shrink living things."

"*Really?*" asked Herby. "What was their purpose?"

"To save the world from the disastrous effects of overpopulation. They think it's the only way to provide enough food and space for animals and the increasing number of people."

"That's Herby's reasoning, too," said Dad. "I feel like such a fool for not taking him seriously when he tried to explain his project to me."

"That's okay, Dad. I admit it did sound pretty unbelievable."

"You'll be going to the largest, private biomedical-research facility in the world, Herby," said Dr. Bloomquist.

"Have they tested their formula on any animals?" asked Herby.

"Yes, on several, including mankind's next-of-kin, the chimpanzee. And here's the best part of it where you're concerned, Herby. They were able to return them all to their previous sizes, with no ill effects from the experience."

"Why haven't we heard about any of this on the news?" asked Dad.

"I asked that very question of Dr. Vanderpool. He said it must be kept secret until it can be discussed at the UN, and a plan developed for its use. Can you imagine what might happen if the formula fell into the wrong hands?"

"Yes," answered Dad. "And with all this publicity about Herby, the secret is out."

"When can we go to San Diego?" asked Herby.

"As soon as possible," answered Dr. Bloomquist.

Dr. Sutton returned to the room with the x-ray negatives and attached them to the light box on the wall. Both he and Dr. Bloomquist studied them intently.

"I'm used to looking at x-rays of teeth," said Dr. Sutton, "but I see nothing here to indicate a fracture."

"I agree," said Dr. Bloomquist. "It appears, Herby, that you just have a badly sprained ankle. Just keep it wrapped until the swelling goes down."

"I'm sure glad it isn't broken," said Herby. "When will I be able to walk on it?"

"Any time. It would be good to exercise it a little. Just don't overdo it."

When Herby and his dad returned home, the street in front of the house was lined with vehicles and people. There were two lawn chairs in the middle of the driveway. Dad had to get out and move them aside so that he could pull the car in.

Grandpa hurried down the porch steps "Quick, John, pull into the garage before these news people descend on you. I'll put the chairs back where I had them."

"That was a good idea," said Dad as he got back into the car. "We need to keep this driveway clear."

Mom met Herby and his dad as they entered the house from the garage. "What did Dr. Bloomquist say? Is Herby's ankle broken?"

"It's just a bad sprain, Mom. The doctor said I can even start walking on it."

"That's great news, Herby. I'm so glad you're back home. There are several people in the den waiting to see you."

"I thought we'd agreed to keep the news people away from Herby until the interview this evening!" said Dad.

"They aren't news people, John. They're people Herby met last week during his ordeal. Bud's in there, too."

Just then, loud banging came from upstairs. "What's going on up there?" asked Dad.

"It's those TV people setting up their equipment. I'm glad you're home to monitor them. Grandpa hasn't been able to. He's been too busy outside, keeping people away from the doors and windows."

"Dad, my recorder and tapes, and all the notes about the formula, are up there in my room," Herby said excitedly.

"Oh, my goodness, that's right! We can't afford to have anything happen to them. I'll go get them and put them in a safe place."

"While you're up there, Dad, would you check on my animals? All that activity in the room might be scaring them."

"Okay!"

Mom carried Herby into the den, and as he glanced around the room, he saw his Uncle Bud and waved. *He brought the old man!* thought Herby. *And there's Bruno!* Herby didn't recognize anyone else. All eyes were on Herby as Mom placed him in his chair in the dollhouse.

"Each of you will have a chance to talk to Herby," she said. "Would you like to start, Detective Clawson?"

"Thank you, Mrs. Strange. This won't take long." The detective pulled his chair up close to the dollhouse. "Hello, Herby, I'm Detective Clawson."

This time, Herby nodded instead of offering to shake hands. "Pleased to meet you, sir."

"I'm sorry to have to bother you and your family at this time, but there's a hearing scheduled for tomorrow. It concerns one of the men who allegedly kidnapped you. We have a statement from Mr. Bruno Braun and one from Mrs. Kate Quinley and her husband Gus. They will also be witnesses at the hearing. It won't be necessary for you to be there, Herby, but a statement from you would be very helpful. Are you able to give us one now?"

"Sure." Herby cleared his throat. "That Jake guy, or whatever his real name is, is a very bad man and deserves to be locked up."

"Thank you, Herby, but we need a little more than that. Could you please start at the beginning and tell us everything that Jake, or whatever his real name is, did from the time you first met him?"

The detective pulled a recorder from his pocket and turned it on. "The following is a statement from the victim, eleven-year-old Herbert Milton Strange, case number 127." He set the recorder next to Herby. "Go ahead, Herby," he said. "Please speak into the recorder as loudly as you can."

All eyes were on Herby...

Herby pointed across the room to Bruno. "That nice man over there tried to help me, and Jake, or whatever his real name is, hit him over the head with a skillet and knocked him out and—"

The detective interrupted. "Excuse me, Herby." He leaned down to speak into the recorder, "The victim is pointing to witness Bruno Braun. Please continue, Herby."

Herby once again told the story of how Jake had kidnapped him, threatened to "squash him like a bug," stole a nice lady's truck, and then tossed Herby into the water to drown.

After Herby had finished speaking, the detective held up a photograph. He said into the recorder, "The victim is now being shown a photograph of the suspect, Archibald Allbad, alias John Smith, alias Jake Jones. Herbert Milton Strange, is this the man who abducted you?"

Seeing Jake's mean, ugly face again made Herby shudder. "Yes, sir! That's him, all right!"

"Thank you, Herby," said the detective as he picked up the recorder and turned it off. "I think we have everything we need. But before I go, I want to say that I think you are an extremely brave young man. My colleagues and I are very impressed with the way you've conducted yourself throughout this entire ordeal."

"Thank you, sir. And thank *you* for helping to make sure Jake, or whatever his real name is, won't hurt anyone else."

While Herby's mom was showing Detective Clawson to the door, the old man walked over and sat down in the chair vacated by the detective. "I was awfully upset when ye ran off the way ye did. But ye sure and begorra came through for me, didn't ye, lad? Ye found me son! Now I'd like ye to meet him." The old man motioned to his son and family. A handsome young man and a pretty woman carrying a baby came to the dollhouse. Herby noticed that both the man and baby had bright red hair.

Uncle Bud joined them, saying, "Mr. O'Sullivan was right where you said he might be, Herby."

"Lad, this is me long-lost son, Grady O'Sullivan. But ye didn't just find me son." The old man put his arm around the shy young woman's waist and pulled her closer. "Look here at me beautiful daughter-in-law, Maggie." The old man reached up to take the baby from the woman's arms and set him in his lap. "And see what this beautiful lass has given me: A fine grandson! They named him Patrick after me."

"I'm glad to meet all of you," said Herby.

The baby had been intently staring at Herby. At hearing Herby speak, the baby lunged at him. Herby fell over in his chair as he dodged the chubby little hand trying to grab him. Herby's mother came into the room, saw what was happening, and screamed. She ran to the dollhouse.

"Herby!" she cried. "Are you hurt?"

Laughing, Herby set the chair back upright and sat back down. "I'm okay, Mom. The baby must have thought I was some kind of toy."

The old man handed the baby back to its mother. "He's an O'Sullivan, all right—just six months old and already causing a commotion."

"I'm sorry I had to run out on you the way I did," said Herby, "but I just couldn't convince you that I wasn't a leprechaun."

The old man winked at Herby. "To tell ye the truth, lad, I'm not convinced yet."

Herby laughed. "Thanks a lot for the clothes you made me, especially the boots. I don't think I could have survived without them."

"The boots! I almost forgot." He reached into his coat pocket and held out a new pair of boots. "Your Uncle Bud said you'd worn out the first pair I made and wished ye had another pair just like them."

"Gee, thanks, Mr. O'Sullivan!" Herby said as he kicked off the ill-fitting doll shoes. He put on one boot, but didn't try to get the other one on over his wrapped foot and ankle. "This one fits just perfect. Pretty soon, I'll be able to wear the other one, too."

"I would have made ye some new clothes, too," said the old man, "but I didn't have time. I had to pack me belongings. I see ye have some nice, new clothes though."

"You had to pack your belongings? Are you going back to Ireland?"

"Pop's moving up to the lake with us," said Grady.

"And you know what else, Herby?" said the old man, grinning, "I've got a new job. I'm going to be in charge of patching up torn sails."

"Pop will be a great asset to our boat repair business," Grady added. "With his sewing skills and equipment, we can add sail repair. There's a big need for that at the lake."

Suddenly, tears welled up in the old man's eyes and spilled out onto his wrinkled cheeks.

"I tell ye, lad, you've made me the happiest man alive. I'll be forever grateful to ye."

As Herby stammered for words, Grady said, "Come on now, Pop. Don't get all blubbery on us." Grady wiped a tear from his own eye. "We've got to go now. We've got a lot of work to do today."

The old man rose from the chair. "Will I be seein' ye again, lad?"

"You can count on it, Mr. O'Sullivan!"

"I'll be leaving now too, Herby," said Uncle Bud. "But I'll be sure to watch you on the news tonight!"

Herby's heart felt all puffed up inside as he waved goodbye to the O'Sullivans.

Bruno came to the dollhouse and sat down in the chair vacated by the old man. "Hi, there, little fella! Am I ever glad you showed up when you did. No tellin' how long those shrinks woulda kept me locked up!"

"How is your head, Mr. Bruno? Jake gave you a pretty good whack with that iron skillet. I was afraid he might have killed you."

"It's a good thing he hit me in the head, or he might have done some damage," said Bruno, chuckling. He tapped the side of his head with his fist. "It would take more'n a skillet to crack this hard ole' noggin."

"I sure thank you for trying to help me, sir."

"I sure didn't though, did I? I shoulda known better than to turn my back on that snake. I hope your mom don't mind that I stopped by to see you, Herby."

"Of course, she doesn't mind. My mom and dad are both grateful to you for trying to help me. And I'm glad you stopped by. You had a lot of trouble because of me. I feel better knowing you're all right."

"They say somethin' good comes out of somethin' bad, little fella. The somethin' bad was that the shrinks wouldn't let me go, and I missed a lot of work. I don't know what woulda become of the diner if my ex-wife, Bessie, hadn't stepped in to keep it open. The somethin' good is that me and Bessie are gettin' back together. Every night after she closed up the diner, she came to see me at the hospital. It was because of you, and that smack on the noggin, that she came back into my life."

"I'm glad I could be of help, Mr. Bruno."

"So long, then, little fella, and good luck! I'll see you on TV!"

Mom escorted Bruno to the door and then addressed the waiting couple. "I'm sorry you've had to wait so long, Mr. and Mrs. Quinley. You may talk to Herby now."

They seated themselves next to the dollhouse. "Hello, Herby," said the man. "We haven't actually met, but we've talked. At least you talked to me. I just couldn't talk back."

"You must be Gus. And you're Kate," Herby said, turning to the woman. "I've been wondering how you were after all that happened."

"I'm fine. I just got a little cold and wet from the rain. But you must have been terrified! It's hard to believe that horrible man had you in his pocket all that time. I wish I had known. I might have been able to do something."

"I don't know what you *could* have done," said Herby. "Jake is a mean and dangerous man. I'm sorry your truck got wrecked. Can it be fixed?"

"I'm afraid not. But thank goodness, it was covered by insurance."

"We've got a brand-new shiny red truck parked a few blocks away," Gus added. "We wanted you to see it, but with all the activity out there, we couldn't find a closer place to park."

"We didn't mean to stay long, Herby," said Kate. "We just wanted to tell you how glad we are that you made it back home. And we hope you get better soon—your size, that is."

"And I wanted to tell you, young man," said Gus, "that was mighty quick thinking on your part to answer my call on the CB radio."

"I wasn't even sure you heard me," said Herby. "But I'm sure glad you did."

Kate rose from her chair. "We should go now, Herby. It's been really nice to see you. Oh, and by the way, I don't pick up strangers on the road anymore."

"Good," said Herby.

"Say, young man, when you've managed to grow some, how would you like a ride in our new truck?" asked Gus.

"I'd like that."

"Good. Then we'll be seeing you again."

Chapter 19

Making
News

Soon after the Quinleys left, Herby heard a commotion on the front porch. He couldn't make out the words, but could hear his grandpa and the loud shrill voice of a woman.

He heard the door open. "What in the world is going on out here?" his mother asked.

"I demand to see either Mr. or Mrs. Strange!" a woman shrieked. "Will you please go get one of them for me?"

"I'm Mrs. Strange. What seems to be the problem?"

"The problem is this stupid, rude, idiotic security guard here!" snapped the woman. "He refuses to let me into the house. Why, he doesn't even know who I am!"

"That security guard happens to be Herby's grandfather, trying to protect our privacy. And just who *are* you?"

"You don't recognize me either? Don't people in this backwoods town own TVs? I'm Natalie Norwood, anchor woman of KNOT News."

"Now that you mention it, you do look somewhat familiar. I'm sorry we didn't recognize you. We don't watch much television."

"May I come in?" asked the woman in a demanding voice.

Before Mom had a chance to answer, the beautiful well-dressed woman entered the den, plopped down in the chair next to the dollhouse, and took a notepad and pen from her purse.

"Ms. Norwood," said Mom, as she followed the woman, "We were assured there'd be no meetings with the media until the scheduled interviews."

"I prefer to first meet with the individuals I will be interviewing," said the woman. "That way I can be better prepared to ask more in-depth questions."

"That doesn't seem fair to the other reporters," said Mom.

"My dear Mrs. Strange, I didn't get where I am today by being fair. Getting the best news first is the name of the game. May we get on with this?"

Now I know what they mean when they say beauty is only skin deep, thought Herby.

"Tell me, Mrs. Strange, does Herby have an adequate vocabulary to express himself? If not, I would form questions so as not to embarrass the child."

"Why don't you ask him yourself?"

"Yes, I need to talk to him right away. Would you please fetch him for me? We don't have much time to prepare."

"Just turn your head to the left," said Mom.

Ms. Norwood glanced at the dollhouse next to her. Puzzled, she asked, "What on earth do you mean, Mrs. Strange?"

"Look more closely."

Herby stood up on one leg and bowed to her.

The woman screamed and jumped out of her chair, flinging the notepad and pencil into the air. The entire contents of her purse spilled out onto the floor. "I thought that was a doll sitting there," she gasped. "I was told he was small. I had no idea he was so—so—*tiny!*"

"I can assure you, Ms. Hardwood," said Mom, "that Herby has quite an extensive vocabulary and he—"

"*Nor*wood is the name!" the woman snapped.

"Oh, yes, Ms. *Nor*wood. Has it occurred to you that were it not for the fact that Herby is a genius, none of this would have happened?"

Herby's mom got down on her knees and began picking up the contents of the woman's purse. Natalie didn't offer to help. Mom finally stood up and handed Natalie her purse.

"Thank you. But where's my notepad?"

Mom found the notepad behind a chair and handed it to the woman.

"Good," said Natalie. "Now we can continue."

"No," said Mom. "We're through here."

Good for you, Mom, thought Herby.

"But we haven't even begun. I—"

Mom took a firm grip on the woman's arm and led her to the door. "Goodbye, Ms. Norwood," said Mom. "Nice meeting you."

As Mom was closing the door, Herby heard the woman sputter, "Well, I never—"

"You didn't really mean that, did you, Mom?"

"Mean what, Herby?"

"That it was nice meeting her."

Mom laughed. "I guess not. But it *was* really nice telling her goodbye."

Mom held out her hand to Herby, palm up. "Everyone is in the dining room waiting for lunch. We'd better get in there."

"It's nice to be important, but it's more important to be nice, huh, Mom?" said Herby as he crawled into her palm.

"Absolutely! And since you are now so important in the eyes of the world, don't ever forget that little saying."

A table and chair from the dollhouse were now the centerpiece for the dining room table.

Herby hobbled over to the little table and took his seat. As they ate, the family chatted back and forth about the morning's events. Grandma asked, "What are those people working upstairs going to do about lunch? Do you suppose I should take them up something to eat?"

"Don't worry about them," answered Dad. "There's a catering truck parked out back in the alley. They're having lunch on the patio, around that big table they carried down from Herby's room."

"Where's Bozo?" asked Herby. "I haven't heard him barking lately."

"That's because he's busy mooching food from all those people he was barking at earlier," said Dad.

"They carried down one of Herby's tables?" asked Mom.

"Yes. One of the producers did some figuring about how many people were going to be in that room during the interviews," said Dad. "It's a big room, but they still needed to take out most of the furniture. It's stacked in our bedroom."

"What happened to all the stuff that was on my big table?" asked Herby.

"I took care of that myself," said Dad. "I boxed it all up and put it in the storeroom."

"I thought this was going to be a simple interview," said Mom, "with just us and two or three news people. Instead, it has turned into a major disruption of our household!"

"Evidently, there's a lot of behind-the-scenes effort," said Dad. "For instance, the lighting and sound have to be just right, and it's been difficult due to Herby's small size."

"Don't forget," said Grandpa, "all the major networks, plus the local networks and radio stations, will each have several people up there."

"Why on earth do they need so many people?" asked Grandma.

"From what I understand," said Dad, "each network has its own reporter, at least one cameraman, and a sound man."

"Dad, how are all my critters up there?" asked Herby.

"They seem to be tolerating all the hubbub okay. I was going to take the cages out of there, but some set director wanted them left. He said the animals would add character to the background."

Early afternoon passed quickly. Herby's scout patrol and several others from his troop stopped by to see him after school. J.C. unloaded some books and papers from his knapsack. "Mr. Smothers asked me to deliver your homework from last week. Looks like you've got a lot to catch up on."

"Homework!" said Herby. "And I thought my troubles were almost over. I don't need my glasses to read, but writing stuff down is going to be a problem."

"Hey, Herby," said Tom, "Debbie keeps asking about you. I bet she'd be real happy to take dictation for you."

"I've always felt weird being around girls my age who were taller than I am," said Herby. "How do you think I'd feel now?"

"That's a point," said Tom. "I guess the boys and I will just have to take turns being your secretary."

The conversation turned toward the scout troop's plans to honor Herby. "Mr. Davidson is planning to have a potluck banquet," said Jeff. "He wants to present you with some awards. He said that with all you went through, you're eligible for a bunch of merit badges."

"Wilderness Survival would definitely be one of them," said Nathan.

"Yeah, Herby," added Tom, "and Plant Science, and Hiking, and—I bet you're even eligible for the 50-miler Award."

"I've never heard of that one," said Clay. "What do you have to do for it?"

"Well, basically, you have to travel for a minimum of five days and cover a minimum of fifty consecutive miles," answered Tom. "You can do it either by walking or in a boat. In Herby's case, he did both. And you can't use a motor."

"I sure *would* have used a motor if I'd had one, though," said Herby. "But I can't qualify for that badge. I only went about fifteen miles."

"Figure it out, Mr. Science," said J.C. "How tall are you? I don't mean now, I mean before."

"Gee, I don't know."

"Well, even if you were six feet tall, and you're what—about six inches now?" asked J.C. "You'd have to travel—does anyone have a pencil?"

Nathan, who was very good at math, already had an answer. He said, "A person six inches tall would be traveling the equivalent of about twelve times farther than one who was six feet tall. So if the little guy traveled fifteen miles, it would be the same as the big guy going about one hundred eighty miles."

"Wow!" the boys said in unison.

"So, Herby, since you weren't even close to being six feet tall, that means you probably went the equivalent of more than two hundred miles," said J.C.

"Does that mean he should get four 50-Miler Awards then?" asked Tom.

The boys were enjoying a good laugh when Mom entered the den. "I'm sorry to interrupt your fun, but Herby's father and I need to have a very important discussion with him right away."

"Thanks for coming, guys," said Herby. "I've been really nervous about this TV thing this evening. I feel better knowing you'll be out there rooting for me."

"You mean we'll be out there *hooting* for you," said Jeff. The boys all began hooting loudly and kept it up as they went marching out the door, whoooo, whoooo, whoooo."

"What was *that* all about?" asked Mom.

"Our patrol is the Hoot Owls, Mom. Don't you remember? What you just heard is our patrol yell."

"Oh, yes, how could I forget?"

Dad entered the den with a serious look on his face. "Herby, that research scientist, Dr. Vanderpool, just called. He said that with all the publicity you're getting, flying to San Diego on a regular airline was not a good idea. He's offered to have the research center's private plane fly you to San Diego."

"That's great, Dad. When do we go?"

"That may be a problem. The plane is on its way back to San Diego from New York and will be refueling in Grand Junction about six thirty this evening. He said if you could be there at that time, you would be in San Diego before morning."

"That's awfully short notice," said Mom. "Can't the pilot stay over tonight in Grand Junction and fly out tomorrow? It's going to take us some time to get ready."

"I suggested that to Dr. Vanderpool," answered Dad, "but the plane has to be in San Diego by early tomorrow morning. It's scheduled to fly one of Dr. Vanderpool's colleagues from there to Dallas for an important fundraising event."

"Well, can't they pick Herby up on their way back from Dallas?"

"Dr. Vanderpool said that if Herby couldn't go this evening, it would be nearly two weeks before they could arrange to pick him up," answered Dad. "The plane will be in use back east until then."

"Gee, Mom," said Herby, "I don't want to be small like this any longer than I have to. I'd like to start working on an antidote as soon as possible."

"I feel the same way," said Mom. "We'll just have to hurry and get ready to go. How long do you think we'll be gone, John?"

"I've been thinking about that. I really can't spare much more time from work. And there's really no need for us both to go to San Diego. I'll drive you to the airport this afternoon and you two go on without me. I'm sure Grandma and Grandpa won't mind staying here a little longer to watch after Suzanne."

"Then it's settled," said Mom. "I'll start packing right now."

"At least I won't have to spend much time packing," said Herby. "I'll be wearing most of *my* clothes. But you'd better pack my school books and homework, Mom."

"I'll pack those for you in my old attaché case," offered Dad, "and your extra boot, too."

"I'll pack all your formula notes and tapes in my big purse," said Mom. "I never lose sight of my purse, so they'll be safe in there."

A noise came from upstairs. "I forgot all about the TV interviews," said Mom. "We certainly don't have time for all that now."

"Maybe I could do just one interview," said Herby. "I'd probably just be answering the same old questions from each one anyway."

Dad thought for a minute. "That just might work. They're planning to start at three o'clock. If you just do one interview, it probably wouldn't take more than twenty minutes."

"What if they don't like that idea?" asked Mom. "They're all so competitive."

"I don't see that they have much choice," answered Dad. "They'll either agree to sharing one interview, or they'll get nothing."

"I'll be upstairs packing," said Mom. "I'll leave you to notify everyone of the change of plans."

Chapter 20

Setting the Stage

D ad called his parents into the den to explain the situation. "Of course, we'll stay," said Grandma.

"We'll stay as long as you need us," said Grandpa. "The important thing is to get our Herby back to normal."

A short time later, Mom returned to the den, carrying a suitcase and an overnight bag. Suzanne followed behind, whimpering, "But why can't I go, too?"

"Don't you want to stay here with Grandpa and me?" asked Grandma.

Suzanne didn't answer. She just looked down at the floor with her lower lip puckered out.

Dad had been upstairs, and came into the den, looking exhausted. "Well, I broke the news to the TV and radio technicians. They're contacting their headquarters now, trying to decide how they're going to work the interview."

"Those TV stars aren't going to be happy about having to share the spotlight, I'll bet," said Grandpa. "They'll all be showing up here pretty soon, too."

Mom looked at her watch. "Oh, my goodness, look what time it is, John. You'd better get dressed. You can't wear that old shirt on television."

Grandpa picked up the luggage. "I'll take these out to the car now, Lisa. John wants to leave the minute the interview is over."

Grandma headed for the kitchen. "I'll go pack some food for you to take. You'll have to eat your supper in the car on the way to Grand Junction."

"Thank you both," said Mom. She looked at Herby. "You're going to have to get dressed for the interview, too, young man, but in what?"

Suzanne looked up from her coloring book. "You don't have to worry about that, Mommy. I have Herby's clothes all laid out upstairs on my bed."

"You didn't tell me you were going to do that. What clothes did you have in mind?"

"I wanted it to be a surprise, but I can't wait. My friend Janie has a Ben doll, and she loaned Herby some of his clothes. They're really gant."

"Really *gant*?" asked Herby.

Mom hugged Suzanne. "I think you mean el-e-gant, don't you, Sweetie?"

"Yes. And they're really nice, too. I'll go get them."

Suzanne soon returned and proudly laid the clothes on Herby's dollhouse bed.

"No way!" said Herby. "It's bad enough that I'm going to be sitting in a doll's chair in a cage in front of a zillion people. I am *not* wearing any tuxedo!"

"Don't be so hasty," said Mom. "You could wear part of it. A white dress shirt and black pants would be very appropriate."

"But the red thing that goes around his stomach, and the little bow tie, and the coat with the long tails, is what makes it so really gant—el-e-gant," whined Suzanne.

"Try the shirt on, Herby," said Mom. "If the clothes fit, I'll wash and dry them while you're getting washed up. If they don't, I hope Marci has something suitable." She turned to Suzanne. "Why don't you call Janie and tell her we thank her for loaning Herby her doll's clothes."

"Yes! And I'll tell her to watch for them on TV!"

The mayor showed up nearly an hour early. "My, don't you look nice!" said Mom as she ushered him into the living room. "I'm helping Herby get dressed, so please make yourself comfortable."

"I'm sorry if I'm a little early," said the mayor. "I'll just read the paper here and—say, you wouldn't happen to have any more of those delicious cookies, would you?"

Meanwhile, Herby was thankful that the Ben doll's clothes fit him fairly well. The pants were a little long, but he could stuff one leg into his new boot. The other, he could wrap up in his ankle bandage. After

Herby bathed and dressed, his mother gently brushed his hair with a new toothbrush. "Go look at yourself in the mirror, Herby. See how nice you look! I'll go invite the mayor into the den now."

...his mother gently brushed his hair with a new toothbrush.

The mayor entered the den, carrying a plate of cookies. He pulled a chair over to the dollhouse and sat down. "You look quite spiffy, young man. Are you excited about all this?"

"Scared is more like it."

"I remember being nervous the first time I spoke in public, but I've gotten used to it."

"I don't plan on getting used to it," said Herby.

Herby's grandparents and Suzanne entered the den, and the mayor stood up to greet them. Grandpa offered his hand. "Good evening, Mayor Farnsworth. I don't believe you've met Herby's sister, Suzanne."

The mayor bowed toward Suzanne. "I'm delighted to meet such a pretty little girl." Suzanne giggled as the mayor returned to his seat.

"Are you going to be on TV, too?" Herby asked his grandparents.

Grandma waved her hand. "Heavens, no! There won't even be room for us to watch you up there. We'll get to see you later, on the six o'clock news. We're just going to stay here in the den and keep Suzanne company."

"But I won't be here," said Suzanne. "I'm going to be on TV!"

Grandma shook her head. "No, dear, it will just be Herby and your parents."

"But that's not fair!" Suzanne cried as she puckered up her face. "Why can't I be on, too?"

"Just what would you do if you *were* on TV?" asked Grandpa.

"My dance! I'm going to do my favorite number from dance class. I've been practicing all day in front of the mirror in Mommy's room! And Janie's going to be watching for me! I'm going to be on TV!"

"I'm sorry, dear," said Grandma. "Not this time."

Suzanne stomped her foot. "We'll just see about that!" She ran from the den, crying.

"Looks like you have a budding performer in the family," commented the mayor.

"She can be pretty headstrong at times," said Grandpa.

Herby heard cars coming and going outside in the street and driveway. Car doors were slamming and people talking.

"Sounds like the news people are arriving," said the mayor.

"Where in the world are they all going to park?" wondered Grandpa.

"Are they all going to be marching through the house to Herby's room?" asked Grandma.

"I have one of our officers stationed in the driveway to meet them," answered the mayor. "The media people were instructed to have a driver who could drop them off here and park elsewhere. People are being directed to the rear of the house and the outside stairs to Herby's room."

"I'm sure glad you took care of that, Mayor," said Grandpa. "I've had my fill of directing people all day."

"Wouldn't it have been easier for them to use the alley instead of the driveway?" asked Grandma.

"I'm afraid not," answered the mayor. "You haven't looked outside lately, have you?"

"Not lately. Seems like every time I peek out from behind the blinds, some nosey peeper is peeking back at me. I just don't know what gets into people!"

"Curiosity, Mrs. Strange. Curiosity."

And I'm the curiosity, thought Herby.

The mayor continued, "They can't use the alley because two big satellite trucks are blocking it. The rest of the alley and the street in front of the house are filled with onlookers."

"It appears the entire town of Mountainview has turned out for this," said Grandpa.

"Not just Mountainview," said the mayor. "Folks are here from all over the state and beyond. There's not an empty hotel or motel room left in town. Some folks are even renting out rooms in their homes. And the restaurants and shops are reporting an extremely brisk business. Why, our police force is working extra shifts just to keep up with the increased traffic. Yes, you people should be proud. Little Herby here has put this town on the map."

The mayor stood up again when Dad entered the room. "Good afternoon, Mr. Strange. Are they ready for us up there?"

"I'm not sure. But they'd better be. We don't have much time."

"No need to rush," said the mayor. "We have plenty of time for all the interviews before they're to be aired at six o'clock."

"There's been a change of plans," said Dad as he walked to the dollhouse. He held the palm of his hand out to Herby. "How about it, Herby, are you ready?"

"I guess so," answered Herby as he hobbled over to his dad's hand and sat down.

"What change of plans?" asked the mayor.

"I'll tell you about it on our way upstairs."

"Where is Suzanne?" asked Grandma.

"She's upstairs in her room pouting," said Dad.

"The poor thing. She really wanted to be on television."

"I have the DVD recorder all set," said Dad. "I'm recording the interview so the rest of us can see it when we get back."

"When you get back?" asked the mayor.

Dad explained the recent change of plans to the mayor as they climbed the stairs.

Mom stepped into the hallway from Suzanne's room. "Herby's room is packed with people and cameras," she said. "Would you mind breaking trail for us, Mayor, by going in first?"

"Why, of course, my dear."

"Coming through!" the mayor announced loudly as he entered Herby's room. So much arguing was going on, that no one seemed to notice them.

"This is the mayor of Mountainview, coming through!" he yelled.

Dad carried Herby clutched against his chest as they made their way through the crowd to the far end of the room. Mom opened the lid of the cage sitting on a table there. Dad removed the dollhouse chair from his pocket and set it inside. After gently lowering Herby onto the chair, Dad shut the lid and secured it.

Herby looked around the inside of the cage. *Seems like I've been here before.*

Mom positioned herself on one side of the table and Dad on the other. "We're ready, Mayor," said Dad. "You can come around behind the table now."

When the mayor stepped aside, those near the front of the room got their first glimpse of Herby. A hush fell over the room, and several gasps were heard. "This has *got* to be some kind of a stunt!" said one. "That *can't* be a real boy!"

The loud talking returned and cameras began flashing.

Herby watched as a well-dressed man made his way toward him through the crowd. *He sure looks familiar,* thought Herby. The man's eyes were intently fixed on Herby as he approached the cage. "Are you for real?" he whispered.

"Sure, I'm for real!" The sound of his own booming voice made Herby nearly jump out of his chair.

"That's a microphone wired to the cage there," said the man, "so everyone can hear you."

"Say, I know you," boomed Herby's voice. "You're Claude Hopper, the top anchorman for KORN, right here in Mountainview!"

The loudly-talking crowd began pressing toward the cage to get a better look at Herby.

"Somebody make them stay back!" cried Mom.

Rising to the occasion, Mayor Farnsworth held up one hand and leaned into the microphone wired to Herby's cage. "Okay, everyone, settle down! Let's have some order. Who's in charge here?"

"That's what we're trying to figure out," called someone from the back of the room.

"The word is we only have time for one interview," said another.

A man wearing headphones and holding a microphone stepped up to the table. "Who are you?" asked the mayor.

"I'm Gregory Allen, a director for TNT," he answered. "All this loud discussion has been about who's going to be the director and which anchor person is going to do the interview. Nothing has been resolved, so there's *no one* in charge here."

"Well, I'll fix that!" said the mayor. He leaned into the microphone. "Listen up, everyone. I'm Mayor Elliott Farnsworth in the running for state representative, and I'll be in charge. I'm appointing

Mr. Allen here to be the director. And Mountainview's own Claude Hopper will conduct the interview."

"Gee, thanks, Mayor," whispered Claude. "This is a great opportunity for me."

"It might as well be you as some outsider," whispered the mayor. "Can you handle it, my boy?"

"You bet! I've already interviewed Herby's neighbors and some of his friends. I know the facts of this story inside and out."

"That unknown person getting all the spotlight is totally unacceptable!" screeched a woman. "Some very important people, myself included, have come a very long way to conduct our own interviews! I demand that we be given the opportunity to do so!"

That voice sounds familiar, thought Herby. *I know! That's Natalie Norwood!*

"You can demand all you want, Missy," answered the mayor. "But it's just not going to happen. Herby and his parents will be leaving in thirty minutes. Now, shall we argue until then, or shall we get on with this interview?"

Gregory Allen, the newly appointed director, said into his microphone, "I think we can make everyone happy. By the time we finish getting set up, we'll only have about twenty minutes left for the interview. Let's see—how many anchors do we have here?" The director quickly looked around the room while counting raised hands. "I'm seeing seven networks— okay, eight. So that's two minutes each of you will have to directly interview Herby. Mr. Hopper, representing local KORN, will begin by conducting a short interview and summary of events."

Herby heard grumbling from the media people. "How about us newspaper reporters?" came a call from the back of the crowd. "Don't we get to ask questions?"

"Any remaining time will be open to any and all who have not yet been heard from," the director answered. "But first, you must raise your hand and wait for my signal."

"We can't see Herby from back here," someone yelled.

"That's what the TV monitors are for. You'll notice there's one near the ceiling on either side of the room." The director turned to his assistant and said, "Let's get those monitors turned on now. Good. How's that, everyone?"

"We can see a cage on the table, but we can't see anything inside," a reporter answered.

"We were waiting to lower the lights over the cage. As you know, they can get uncomfortably hot." The director turned to his assistant. "It's almost time. Lower the lights, and turn them on."

Blinding light suddenly enveloped Herby. As he sat there blinking, he thought, *I'll say those lights are hot. I could get fried here.*

"Is that better?" the director asked. "Can you see him on the monitors now?"

"It's better," someone answered, "but he's so small, he's still hard to see."

"Camera one, zoom in," said the director.

"It's close in here and getting awfully warm," someone called. "Can we open a window or something?"

The director was standing next to the door leading to the outside stairs. He opened it halfway. "That should help. Are we ready now?"

"We *do* have a problem, here," said the mayor.

"What's the problem?" asked the director.

"The lights over the cage are blocking my view."

The director looked puzzled. "What does it matter that you can't see the cameras?"

"It isn't that," answered the mayor. "The cameras can't see *me*."

"We're out of time," said the director as he climbed up and stood on a stool in the corner. "Can everyone see my signals from up here?" he asked. "Good." He looked at his watch. "Quiet, everyone! Stand by! Is the sound ready?"

"Ready," answered an assistant.

Chapter 21

Action!

"Interview with Herby Strange. Ready in 5—4—3—2—" shouted the announcer. He pointed to Claude Hopper and said, "Action! You're on!"

"Good evening ladies and gentlemen. I'm Claude Hopper of channel KORN. We're coming to you from the small but great town of Mountainview in Colorado. There are very few people in the world who, by this time, have not heard of Herby Strange. Like his hometown, he is also small, but great."

How corny can you get, thought Herby.

Stepping aside from the front of Herby's cage, Claude said, "And here he is, folks, the most outstanding scientific wonder of his time—an incredibly large mind in an incredibly small body, Herby Strange!"

Squinting, Herby looked out from between the bars of his cage. Cameras were all lined up, aiming at him. Herby felt like he was before a firing squad.

"Can you say hello to the audience, Herby?" asked Claude.

Herby swallowed hard. "Hello," he said.

"Perhaps he didn't hear me," said Claude, smiling into the TV cameras.

"Will you please say hello, Herby?"

"Hello, again," said Herby.

"I don't understand this," Claude said to the cameras. "He seems to have lost his voice. Perhaps it's just a little stage fright." He leaned down to Herby. "*Please*, Herby," he whispered, "say something!"

"I'm talking as loud as I can," said Herby. "Is there something wrong with the microphone?"

"The microphone?" asked Claude. "Sorry, folks," said Claude, looking back at the cameras. "We seem to be having technical difficulties. We'll be speaking with Herby as soon as we get the trouble cleared up. In the meantime, let me show you the room where it all began."

The director motioned for the crowd to step aside as the cameras followed Claude to one side of the room. The director and his assistant rushed to Herby's cage. "What the devil happened to this microphone?" the director whispered to his assistant.

"It must have come unplugged," said the assistant. Trying to keep out of the field of view of the cameras, he got down on his hands and knees and followed the cord. He returned a few seconds later, holding up the cord's frayed end. "Some furry animal over there in one of the cages chewed the darned thing clean in two," he said. "Whatever that animal was, it didn't do him any good either."

"Oh, no!" cried Herby. "Was the animal white with orange and black spots?"

"It's more like one big black spot now," the assistant whispered.

"Sorry about that, Herby, but we can't dwell on it now," said the director. He said to the assistant, "Go talk to the sound people and see if we can round up another microphone. And make it quick!"

The cameras followed Claude, still talking, back toward Herby where the assistant was quickly attaching a new microphone to Herby's cage. Claude stopped and looked into the camera. "And that, folks, is the setting wherein this boy wonder's imagination was allowed to blossom, flourish, and create his totally remarkable formula."

Seeing the assistant move away from the cage, Claude continued toward it. "And now, we will talk to Herby Strange himself." Claude leaned over the cage. "Herby, do you know you're being referred to as a super colossal genius? How do you feel about that?"

Herby felt himself blushing and lowered his head. "Gosh, I'm just sort of your ordinary, everyday kind of genius."

"My Boy, you're not only a genius, but a very brave one," continued Claude. "In your own words, tell us about the frightful events that transpired from the time you accidentally shrunk yourself."

Herby was surprised that telling his story in front of all the people and cameras came so easily. But he had told it so many times before that it was like he had rehearsed it. He was at the part of the story where Jake wrecked Kate's truck, when he thought he heard someone singing. As the singing became louder and louder, Herby had trouble trying to keep from being distracted as he spoke. He suddenly recognized the voice and the small voice singing, "If you go out in the woods today, you'd better not go alone—it's lovely out in the woods today, but— *That's Suzanne singing her favorite dance piece, The Teddy Bears' Picnic*, thought Herby. *What is she up to?*

Suzanne suddenly popped out of the murmuring crowd and into the lights of the cameras. She continued singing as she twirled around and around in her frilly little dance costume. *Oh, no!* thought Herby as his mouth dropped open.

"Suzanne! Get over here this instant!" Mom whispered. From the tone of her mother's voice, Suzanne knew not to argue. She went to her mother and started to say something. Mom put her hand over Suzanne's mouth and whispered, "Hush!"

The director gave Claude a signal. "And what happened after the accident, Herby?" asked Claude.

Herby faced the cameras and took up his story where he left off. He was at the part where he was crossing Blue Devil Lake on *Can-do*, when he heard a crash. Someone had accidentally knocked over one of the animal cages. Suddenly, there was a blood-curdling scream.

"It's a snake!" someone yelled. "There's a huge rattlesnake loose in here!"

"That's not a rattlesnake!" yelled Herby. "That's my pet bull snake, Wilma. Don't hurt her!" But there was so much turmoil in the room, that no one seemed to pay any attention to his words.

Bozo was lying on the outside stairs landing with his nose just inside the half-opened door. When he heard the scream and ensuing commotion, he charged into the room, barking loudly. He stood by the table, guarding Herby, and continued barking at the unruly crowd.

Natalie Norwood dashed past Herby's cage, still screaming. She ran to the corner behind Herby, where the director stood, seemingly frozen atop his stool. "No!" the director yelled. "Stay down! There's not room for both of us up here!" The mayor quickly pulled Herby's mom and Suzanne out of the way as the director, Natalie, and the stool came crashing down.

"That does it!" Dad growled. "We're getting out of here, *now*!" The people at the other end of the room were bunched up at the door to the upstairs hallway, all trying to leave the room at once. Holding Herby's cage under one arm, Dad guided Mom and Suzanne toward the door to the outside stairway. The boys in Herby's patrol had been sitting on the landing and stairs, listening to Herby's interview. Now they were crowded around the door, trying to see what all the hubbub was about.

The mayor quickly pulled Herby's mom and Suzanne out of the way...

"Make way, boys," cried Dad. "We're coming through!"

As others behind them shoved their way toward the door, Mom cried, "They're all hysterical! If we get on the stairs, they may knock us down."

Dad yelled to Bozo, "Make them stay, Bozo!"

Bozo knew just what to do. Facing into the room, he braced himself at the doorway. The hair on the nape of his neck stood straight up. Growling fiercely, Bozo snarled and snapped at anyone trying to get out the door.

The boys pressed against the railing as Herby, his parents, and Suzanne made their way past them down the stairs. "Hey, Herby!" called J.C. as they passed, "What's up? Where are you going?"

A policeman was working crowd control outside the house and had heard Natalie's scream. He came running to the stairway just as Herby's family reached the bottom. "Stop right there," he said. "What's going on here?"

"We're the Strange family, Officer, Herby's parents," said Dad. "We had to get out of there for our children's safety. Will you please keep the crowds away until we can all get in the car and leave?"

"You say you're leaving with Herby? Where is he?"

Dad held up the cage. "Here I am, Officer," said Herby.

Herby thought the policeman's eyes were going to pop right out of his head. "Holy mackerel! No wonder everyone is making such a fuss about this boy!"

"Can we go now, Officer?" asked Dad. "We have a plane to catch."

"Uhhh, sure! I'll hold off the crowd and radio the officer in front of the house to clear the way for you."

"Thank you, Officer."

The boys in the patrol followed after Herby and his family. "Hey!" said the policeman. "Where do you boys think *you're* going?"

"Dad," said Herby, "May I talk to the boys for just a minute?"

"It's okay, Officer," Dad called over his shoulder. "They're my son's friends."

"Dad!" said Herby. "What about Bozo?"

"I almost forgot!" said Dad. He put two fingers in his mouth and let out a piercing whistle. Bozo was down the stairs and at Dad's feet in a flash. "Thank you, Bozo," said Dad. "Good job!" Herby heard shouting and stomping as people scrambled out of his room and down the outside stairway.

Once the family and boys were inside the garage, Dad locked the door to the backyard. "Whatever you have to say to your friends, Herby, make it quick. We have to get going."

Herby stuck his head through the bars of the cage and looked at his friends crowded around. "I don't have time to explain everything to you now, but it might be quite a while before I see you all again. And I hope to be back to my normal size when I do see you again. My grandparents can fill you in on the details. I just want to thank you for all you've done. I couldn't ask for any better friends."

"We're sure going to miss you," said Jeff.

"Write or e-mail us if you can," said Clay.

"We'll look after all your critters for you," said Tom.

"Will you please put Wilma back in her cage when it's safe to go back up in my room?" Herby asked.

"Sure thing," answered Tom.

"We'll send you your homework assignments so you don't get behind," said Nathan.

J.C. tried to say something, but couldn't quite get it out. A tear ran down his cheek.

Herby waved good-bye to the boys as Dad set his cage in the back seat. When Dad turned to pick up Suzanne, Bozo hopped into the SUV, over the back seat, and hunkered down among the luggage. Dad set Suzanne in the seat next to Herby. He fastened her seat belt and then Herby's around his cage.

Just as Dad got in the front seat beside Mom, the door to the house opened. Herby's grandparents slipped into the garage and shut the door behind them.

Grandma handed a basket to Dad through the car window. "Here's your dinner. We have to get right back in the house. The living room is full of people who came down the stairs from Herby's room. A police officer is keeping them there until you've gone. They're all pretty upset, but I passed out some of my cookies and they seem to be settling down somewhat."

"Thanks for everything," said Dad. "Suzanne and I should be home before 9:30." He punched the remote button, and the garage door noisily began to lift.

Grandpa poked his head in the rear window. "I know you're going to do just fine, Herby. I'm sure you'll be back to normal the next time we see you."

As the car backed out of the driveway, Suzanne turned to her brother. "Don't worry, Herby. If you can't get back to your normal size, you and Marci can get married and live in her nice house happily ever after!"

I can think of only one thing that would be worse, thought Herby. *That would be if some madman got hold of the formula and used it to take over the world.*

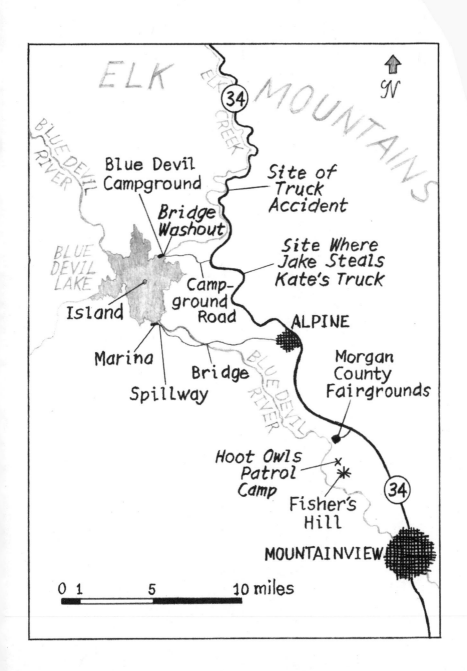

ELK MOUNTAINS

BLUE DEVIL RIVER

34

ELK CREEK

Blue Devil
Campground

Site of
Truck
Accident

*Bridge
Washout*

BLUE
DEVIL
LAKE

Site Where
Jake Steals
Kate's Truck

Camp-
ground
Road

Island

ALPINE

Marina

BLUE DEVIL RIVER

Morgan
County
Fairgrounds

Bridge

Spillway

Hoot Owls
Patrol
Camp

34

Fisher's
Hill

MOUNTAINVIEW

0 1   5   10 miles

About the Author/Illustrator

Sue C. (Strange) Hughey was born in Oklahoma and reared in Kansas. She was a Liberal Arts major at Wichita University, where her father was an art professor. Her mother was a poet and an elementary school teacher in Wichita. After moving to Colorado with her husband Harold and two young sons, Sue worked for several Denver-area art studios and printing companies as a freelance artist and copywriter. She later opened her own graphic arts studio, which evolved into a mapping business, drafting maps for various U.S. Governmental agencies. During this time, Sue contracted with the Environmental Protection Agency to write and illustrate a booklet about the environment, which was distributed to over 60 million school children in the United States. Canada was granted permission to also print and distribute the booklet in that country. Sue also wrote and illustrated a series of educational "map posters," which had a large school market. The coin she designed for Colorado's Centennial, through an act of congress, became the first commemorative medallion ever minted in a U.S. mint (in Denver). She also designed Colorado's commemorative Bicentennial coin, produced by the Franklin Mint. Now retired and living in western Colorado, Sue devotes her time to her first love, writing and illustrating for children.